The Mice Will Play

Also by Edward O. Phillips:

Sunday's Child
Buried on Sunday
Sunday Best

Where There's a Will
The Landlady's Niece

The Mice Will Play

Edward O. Phillips

The Riverbank Press

Canadian Cataloguing in Publication Data

Phillips, Edward, 1931 –
    The mice will play

ISBN 1-896332-03-X (bound)   ISBN 1-896332-05-6 (pbk.)

I. Title.

PS8581.H567M53   C813'.54   C96-931644-5
PR9199.3.P45M53

The Riverbank Press
10 Wolfrey Avenue, Toronto, Ontario M4K 1K8 Canada

Printed and bound in Canada by Métrolitho

for K.S.W.

One

orty-five is a difficult birthday for a woman, especially if she is beautiful. I dealt with mine by ignoring it completely and consigning that particular March day to oblivion. On the unfortunate anniversary of my birth I crossed an international dateline of the spirit, and the day simply disappeared. As a result I am now forty-four for as long as it takes to get my life back on track.

As if the ineluctable truth of having been around for nearly half a century wasn't bad enough, I now had to deal with a serious crimp in the cash flow. Poor dear Walter, the very soul of generosity when he was alive, had postponed making a permanent settlement for that bleak prospect known as my old age. I had brought the subject up from time to time, but I didn't want to press too hard. One doesn't wish to seem greedy; and certain men, lavish with *ad hoc* handouts, can turn quite mulish when faced with the prospect of tying up money for the long term. Besides, neither of us even remotely suspected he would meet such an untimely end.

He appeared to be in the most florid good health on that last afternoon when he came to my apartment instead of attending the directors' meeting pencilled in on his calendar. The jeweller's box he produced from his inside jacket pocket held the most exquisite rope of pearls I had ever seen, each pea-sized sphere identical in size to its neighbours. I have always disliked graduated pearls; they are so depressingly matronly. You really have to be the queen of someplace or other to get away with graduated pearls.

But the rope Walter presented to me positively glowed, its radiance mute testimony to all those irritated oysters working overtime. Pearls have soul, unlike gemstones which offer merely sparkle and spirit. And on my milky, translucent skin they became the stuff of fantasy, of beauty which knows no price.

Wishing to demonstrate my appreciation the best way I knew how, I unpinned my Titian hair—the real thing I hasten to add, untouched by tint or dye. Wearing only the pearls around my neck, I proceeded to give dear Walter one of my magical lingual massages, beginning with the temples and moving slowly down past nipples to that agreeable appendage which has brought me so much profit and pleasure. How could either of us have known that during those few seconds of mystical, if convulsive, union his heart would simply stop.

I did the decent thing: I pulled up the sheet to cover the body and, instead of dialling 911, I telephoned the wife. I explained in simple declarative sentences what had happened, then suggested I was prepared to handle the scandal, but was she? I hardly had time to dress before the wife appeared at my door, in a brown jersey dress and a double string of graduated pearls. I wanted to suggest she would look quite striking as an ash blond, but perhaps then was not the ideal time.

She moved in and took charge, very efficiently I hasten to add. I had gathered, from remarks Walter let drop, that she was an accomplished woman, capable of almost anything but pleasing her husband in bed. She disliked things in her mouth, even gum. I must say I found her rather unfriendly, considering how I had made it possible for Walter's name, and by extension hers, to be kept out of the newspapers. She barely spoke to me, beyond what was absolutely necessary; she cut me dead at the funeral; and she did not even invite me to the reading of the will, although as it turned out, Walter had made no provision whatsoever for me.

The outcome of all this intense activity took a little while to sink in. I genuinely missed Walter, and in my own way grieved over his death. I was sorry he could not have seen how marvellous I looked at the funeral service; he always fancied me in black. Perhaps I should admit, albeit reluctantly, that I had not been in love with Walter. It is never a good idea to fall in love with the man who is paying the bills. Love makes you vulnerable; it causes you to lose perspective. But I had been very fond of Walter. I sincerely regretted his absence, and I very much regretted the absence of his money.

It had been Walter's idea for me to take this expensive apartment, on which rent was now due. I readily complied with his request. Who wouldn't prefer a handsome old apartment with interesting alcoves, large windows, and high ceilings, to a one-bedroom efficiency cube with all the charm of a shoebox. Better still, he wanted me to give up my job. I almost tripped in my eagerness to hand in my resignation as nurse to an upper echelon executive recovering from a broken shoulder. This partially disabled manager was forever feeling me up with his good hand, but he turned out to be a terrible tightwad; the kind of man who gives stinginess a bad name. All I got from him was a sapphire ring, so tiny you needed a loupe to see the stone. It was the kind of ring you wear to the supermarket, on Monday morning.

I have always detested working for a living. A job is joyless and time consuming, so much so that North America has turned work into a virtue in an attempt to sell it to the masses. I am not a lazy woman, but holding down a job had prevented me from devoting time to activities I wanted to pursue full time: cooking, reading, and sex. So when Walter suggested I give up earning my daily bread to live off the fat of the land, I happily complied. Was he not, after all, simply paying me for my time? To my enormous relief, Walter was a twenty-four carat chauvinist; he did not want his very good friend to work. (We never used the word "mistress," so hideously old fashioned. Mistresses wear satin peignoirs, sip champagne cocktails and sit meekly around the apartment all day hoping he'll call.)

For a woman who is having a second try at forty-four and who has spent the last twenty-five years feathering her nest, the prospect was bleak. True, the nest had been well feathered. I studied my beautiful pair of James Wilson Morrices, my Matisse drawing, the Tiffany lamps, the handsome Chippendale highboy—their charm made all the more poignant by the idea they might have to be sold. I also had a safety deposit box holding some very good jewellery, including the rope of pearls. I have never considered jewels as adornment but as security. It would no more occur to me to wear a valuable ruby pendant on the street than to pin a stock certificate to the front of my dress.

Surrounding me were all the obvious accoutrements of gracious living: paintings, furniture, clothes. But a number of bills, which, were he alive, Walter would have paid, had fallen due. My bank account was overdrawn and my credit cards were snapping at my heels like terriers. I had no prospects. Not a single potential admirer stood silhouetted on the horizon. As infinitely dreary and discouraging as it seemed, I had to find a job.

Everybody ought to have a friend like Edith Cross. I honestly don't know how I would have managed without her over the years. I am certainly not the first to observe that opposites attract, but Edith and I are not in the least alike. We are both women, and we both speak English. The resemblance ends there.

An interesting feature of our friendship is that each of us thinks the other terribly old fashioned. We have never discussed the matter openly; there has been no need. Edith has lived the kind of life I knew at sixteen was not for me: a long, monogamous marriage to a good, dull man who never raised his voice, changed his routine, or looked at another woman. They raised three children of sterling character, now making their own ways in the professions of law, medicine, and architecture. She diligently nursed her husband through a lengthy terminal illness. His death left her rich, to use a word my own mother thought vulgar. Edith has no wish to remarry, not even to have the occasional man in her life. Her one true passion is bridge.

Over the years Edith has managed to suggest, always with infinite tact, that women who are prepared to live off their charms belong to an endangered species. Like the black rhino or the Japanese crane we are on our way to extinction. She does not disapprove of my accepting money from men, but rather of the tenuous nature of the transaction. Edith believes in security, in mortgages paid off and dividends arriving quarterly. She is convinced that income should be determined by calendar and computer, not the whims of the latest admirer. She would like me to forsake the world of Marcel Proust for that of John O'Hara. I would not exchange my life for hers, except for the money; and I know without having to be told she feels the same way about mine.

Still, whenever I need a bit of cheering up I call Edith and suggest lunch. We decided on an Italian restaurant, although she never eats anything but clear soup and salad at noon. I was still in mourning—for Walter, for my bank balance, for my prospects—so I decided on black silk. Black does wonders for my hair, and silk feels so good against my skin.

However down I may have felt, I was not defeated, so I allowed myself a little *décolletage*. Even tucking my shoulder-length hair under a broad brimmed hat failed to suggest a woman in the throes of grief. I looked and felt just a bit bare. On my way to the restaurant I stopped off at the bank and took the rope of pearls from my safety deposit box. I wore the pearls in memory of poor dear Walter. And they did help make the neckline of my black silk a little less startling.

Edith was already seated in the restaurant when I arrived. From the entrance I could see those expensively dowdy earth tones, the splendid hair tamed into a bun, glasses hiding beautiful eyes.

"Sorry to be so late, darling." I leaned over to kiss her cheek, stopping half an inch short of the actual surface and making small, chirping noises, like someone talking to a squirrel. "I had an errand at the bank."

"Are we going to throw caution to the winds and have a drink, or split the difference and have some wine?"

"Let's have both. Today is not the day for prudence." I teased my chinchilla jacket over the back of my chair.

We ordered Bloody Marys from a hovering waiter.

"Okay, Gemma," began Edith without preamble. "What's up? When you telephone at ten a.m. suggesting lunch I know you want to talk."

"You're right," I replied. "Life is just a bowl of cherry pits." Upon which I launched into my tale of woe. Edith already knew about Walter's death; an obituary verging on hagiography had filled one quarter of the page devoted to Births and Deaths. But she did not know I was on the verge of being turned onto the street with my Morrices, my Matisse, the Tiffany lamps, and the Chanel suits in a shopping cart. That is unless I went to work.

"What do you intend to do?" she asked between bites of the celery stalk *cum* swizzle-stick from her Bloody Mary.

"What indeed. Unfortunately I have reached an age when most firms don't want to hire me. They want at least twenty-five years of blood, sweat, and tears before paying out a penny of pension. I could go back to full-time nursing, but it's hard work. I've gotten out of the habit of being on my feet. I suppose I could work as a receptionist, announcing in a plummy voice that the doctor will see you now. Could I really stand around an antique store all day assuring *nouveau-riche* matrons in mink coats and costume jewellery that the Coalport platter they are fingering is an absolute steal at the price? Perhaps I could sell clothes in a boutique. 'Believe me, *madame*, that striped lamé makes a statement you simply cannot ignore.'" I shrugged my shoulders in defeat. "I don't know, Edith. I just don't know."

Edith took a thoughtful sip of her drink before answering. "Gemma, what you have failed to do is to analyze your particular abilities. Anybody can work as a receptionist, or a saleswoman. That is not your *métier*. So far you have built a career, a secondary career if such it may be called, on a talent to please. Not everybody has this gift. As a matter of fact, the ability to please is granted to very few. Why not take this enviable asset and turn it to really good use?"

I took a sip of my drink and waited for the point I knew she was about to make.

"I happen to know there are quite a number of older people who require companionship. They do not yet need a trained attendant. And for whatever reasons, they are reluctant to move into a senior citizens' residence."

"Stop right there, Edith. I have absolutely no intention of dealing with bibs and bedpans."

"Hear me out, Gemma." Edith leaned across the table. "I know a woman—she is a member of my bridge circle—who is desperately looking for a companion for her mother. Christine, Christine Blake—she's my bridge partner—is booked for a two week cruise on one of those floating second-class hotels that bobs from island to island in the Caribbean. But she has an elderly mother who needs care during that time. The old lady is hale and hearty, despite her advanced years, but she cannot be left alone in a large house. Christine had engaged a woman to take care of her mother, but she has just backed out, leaving Christine stranded. If she can't find a replacement very soon she will have to cancel her cruise."

Edith paused for a sip of her Bloody Mary. "It would only be for two weeks, and the work won't be hard: helping the old lady to wash and dress; watching a bit of daytime TV; meals on a tray; a few games of double solitaire—nothing really strenuous. You'd be making it up as you go along."

"It sounds beyond ghastly, Edith. I'd sooner go to work as a char." In sheer exasperation I yanked off my hat, allowing my spectacular hair to tumble about my face and shoulders.

"One word of advice," cautioned Edith, "if you decide to go for the interview I suggest you dress down a bit. Wear something with a high neck. Tie your hair back. Not too much eye makeup."

"Look drab in other words."

"You couldn't look drab if you tried. Just tone it down a bit. I am not being fulsome when I say you are beautiful, and many women find real beauty a threat. You would be taking care of an old lady, not a randy stockbroker. And now perhaps we'd better order. I'll have the salad. I've already had my soup."

Ordinarily I would have ordered the salad as well. Mother used to say that if a woman doesn't watch her figure no one else will either. But I needed the comfort of carbohydrates.

"Fettucini Alfredo," I said to the waiter, smiling and opening my green eyes wide.

He smiled back. I have that effect on men. The straight ones want to get me into bed. The gay ones want to do my hair. Either way it's nice to be noticed.

Two

*O*ver the telephone Christine Blake gave me careful instructions on how to get to her house by bus, a lengthy procedure involving at least one transfer and a three block uphill walk. Quite possibly my reduced circumstances would condemn me to taking the bus on a regular basis, a prospect I did not welcome. The bus is for students, pensioners, and those who work by the hour. I never drive myself anywhere, having decided at seventeen that if there was no one to chauffeur me to my destination and if it was too far to walk, I simply would not go. At one point in my past, while seeing an Arab oil magnate, I had a chauffeur driven limousine at my disposal. But the magnate himself had a marked preference for every orifice except the obvious one. I was not sorry to see him go, only a few hours ahead of the police as it turned out; but I sorely missed the limousine.

As I did not wish to arrive hot and flustered for the interview, I took a taxi. My destination lay near the very top of the Westmount mountain. 27 Buckingham Gardens was the address written on a folded piece of paper tucked into the pocket of my cloth coat. At the last minute I decided against carrying a handbag. Shoes and handbags are a sure indication of the wearer's economic status. Since I owned no cheap purses I did not want to spoil my chances by putting down a bag which had set one of my admirers back several hundred dollars. My Patek Philippe watch with the malachite face was tucked safely out of sight under the long sleeved beige blouse with the Peter Pan collar I had bought just for the interview. I wore my hair in a roll around my head. The look had been fashionable a few years ago; now it looked a bit frumpy. The skirt of my most conservative suit completed the outfit, along with a pair of penny loafers, relics of a liaison with a Harvard trained CEO who I had once nursed privately after he broke his leg skiing.

27 Buckingham Gardens, a rambling red brick structure, had been built during the early part of the century when land, labour, and construction materials were all cheap, and nobody stinted on space. I suppose you could have called the building Victorian, although its crenellated tower, Tudor chimneys, formal walk flanked by shrubs still wrapped in burlap against the winter cold, and aluminum storm doors defied easy classification. Warm March sun had melted most of the snow on the front lawn, but shady areas around the house still harboured pockets of stubborn granular ice, like concrete.

The cab had driven away, leaving me marooned in front of the house. With some trepidation—to think I was about to be scrutinized as possible companion for someone's aged mother —I walked up the path and rang the bell.

A woman with features like pastry dough opened the front door. She stood, staring sullenly. Ugly women always dislike me on sight.

"Good morning," I said loftily. "Is Mrs. Blake at home? I believe she is expecting me."

By way of reply the woman moved her starched white uniform to one side, indicating I was to enter. Leaving me to wait in a spacious front hall, she went in search of her employer. I glanced around. An inlaid Empire commode with matching mirror faced a carved oak bench, with a hinged seat allowing it to serve as a chest. Between two doors stood a handsome grandfather clock which did not flaunt its mechanism through glass doors. Good pieces, wildly mismatched.

A woman looking as though she had stepped right from a page in *Town & Country* came down the wide staircase with the loose, rangy stride of one who plays a lot of golf and tennis.

"I am Christine Blake," she announced as if reading the news on television. "How do you do?"

"Gemma Johnstone." She enclosed my hand in a powerful grip. I was glad I wasn't wearing rings.

"Shall we go into the living room, Mrs. Johnson?"

"That's Johnstone, with a 't.' And I'm not married."

"Please take off your coat and sit down. Would you like coffee?"

"Yes, please."

Her departure to give the order gave me a chance to take stock of my surroundings. The room had been furnished in the haphazard fashion that those who inherit good furniture tend to perpetrate. Taken individually, every piece in the room had merit, but nothing went with anything else. A stout Morris chair upholstered in tweed balanced a *bergère* covered in patterned silk. The French provincial couch faced a Tudor oak bench which served as coffee table. Above a heavily carved and varnished mantelpiece hung a gilt framed painting, almost three dimensional so thick was the paint, of "Sunset in the Rockies."

The presence of money was abundantly evident, coupled

with a total absence of style or concept. Rooms tend to reflect their owners, and this particular *salon* suggested that the residents paid scant attention to the niceties of life, an impression only reinforced by the sullen domestic who had opened the door.

Christine Blake strode into the living room. "Coffee will be along in a minute. Do take a seat."

I eased myself into the Morris chair after folding my coat and draping it over the back. Mrs. Blake took the couch. In spite of her casual look I could tell she was a woman preoccupied with her appearance. Tall, big boned, with large hands and feet, she had the gaunt, taut look of someone who has replaced religion with dieting. In every woman's life there comes a time when she must choose between her face and her fanny. Christine Blake had chosen to minimize the latter, with the result that her face, which must once have been beautiful, seemed too tightly stretched over the skull beneath. An extra five pounds would have turned her from arresting into handsome; ten to fifteen would have gone a long way towards restoring her now ravaged beauty. But I have met enough serious dieters to know they burn with the hard gemlike flame of fanaticism, reluctant even to take communion because of the calories in the wafer.

"Edith Cross tells me you are interested in working as a companion," she began. "Have you ever done this kind of work before?"

"Never."

"Then you don't have references." She made the statement as though she had just scored a point in a tennis match. I could see her mentally subtracting dollars from whatever salary she may have had in mind.

"Has your mother ever had a companion?" I asked, keeping my voice casual.

"No, she hasn't."

"Then she has no references either. I realize that in theory the patient is under the care of the companion, or nurse as the case may be. In reality, however, the companion is usually at the mercy of the patient. I am prepared to waive your mother's lack of references if you will overlook mine."

The arrival of coffee gave Mrs. Blake a chance to digest what I had said. I could tell she liked deference from servants, and I had failed to tug my forelock.

The cook put the tray down heavily on the oak bench and shuffled out in white, rubber soled shoes which seemed too full of feet.

"How do you like your coffee?"

"Black, please." I suppose I should have risen from my chair and taken the cup from her hand, but I was not being interviewed to wait on the daughter; furthermore, as I had not yet been hired I remained a guest in her house. I kept my eyes on my demurely folded hands until she rose, crossed to where I sat, and put the cup down onto a pie crust occasional table.

"Thank you," I said.

Mrs. Blake decided the time had come to take charge. "Do you know first aid?" she demanded. I could not tell whether the angle of her chin signalled aggression or merely an attempt to minimize crepe.

"You mean like the Girl Guides? How to make a splint from a field hockey stick or a sling from your troop scarf? No, I don't. But I am an R.N. And I have no compunction about dialling 911 in case of a real emergency."

Christine Blake paused for a sip of coffee. Obviously the interview was not going the way she had anticipated. "What do you expect in the way of salary?"

"Before we even discuss salary, why don't we wait until we see whether or not your mother likes me? If she doesn't, there is no point in my even considering the job. If she does, we will have to work out what my duties will be, a job description, as they say in industry."

I could see Christine Blake beginning to bristle, but she had to admit, albeit reluctantly, that I had a point.

"One last question, Miss Johnson . . . "

"It's Johnstone, with a 't.'"

"Can you cook? Will you be able to deal with Mother's meals? Unfortunately Cook has given her notice. She leaves at the end of the week to look after a sick sister. I don't want to go about finding a replacement until I get back from my cruise. So you will have to prepare Mother's meals while I am away."

"In all modesty, Mrs. Blake, I can say I'm an excellent cook. If your mother is at all like other elderly people I have known, she has a small appetite. That means she would prefer a variety of small portions, properly cooked and attractively served. On that score you need have no concern."

"Very good, Miss Johnstone. I have charge accounts at all the local stores, and they all deliver. Now, why don't I take you upstairs to meet Mother?"

"If it's all the same to you, Mrs. Blake, I would prefer to go up by myself. That way your mother and I can meet without manipulation of attitudes. Were you to take me upstairs you would say something like, 'Mother, this is Gemma Johnstone; she is going to be your companion. She's a good friend of Edith Cross, with whom I play bridge. I'm sure you two will get along just splendidly.' Your mother will probably look at me with deep and instant dislike, and I will never be able to overcome that initial negative impression. I would prefer to meet her alone."

I stood, indicating the interview had come to an end. "Now, what room is she in? Is there anybody who might be embarrassed to meet me on the stairs?" For just a second Christine Blake hesitated, probably torn between a desire to throw me into the street and the realization that I was more than likely right.

"She's in the tower room, up two flights of stairs and then another short flight on the right. And everybody's out at the moment. While you are up there you can decide which of the rooms on the third floor you would like to use, and I will have the cleaning woman do it up for you."

"I beg your pardon?" I said, astonished by the idea that I would be expected to live in.

"The room—which you will use during your stay. You can go out for short periods during the day, but Mother cannot be left alone at night. And now that Cook is leaving, the house will be otherwise empty. Didn't Edith make that clear?"

"Not entirely," I replied, collecting myself and forcing a smile. "But it stands to reason your mother not be left alone." I headed for the staircase. I know stairs are supposed to be good for the calves and the heart, but with two flights and a bit every time the old lady needed something I would definitely require a salary supplement.

My way lay up the staircase Christine Blake had descended like a showgirl gone to seed. I climbed the handsome oriental runner, held in place by brass rods, to the second floor, where the hall itself was spacious enough to serve as an upstairs sitting

room. Assorted armchairs and a camel-backed sofa had been upholstered with a kinetic chintz in an unsuccessful attempt to pull
it all together.

I continued my ascent up a plain beige runner with the
telltale sheen of synthetic pile. Only the very wealthy are given
to cutting corners like putting down a good wool runner where
it shows, then switching to cheaper quality where the general
public does not go. I would have been willing to bet Christine
Blake used top-of-the-line toilet paper in the ground floor toilet,
and a cheaper brand—eight rolls to the package—in the family
bathrooms.

At the top of the second flight of stairs a door to the right
opened onto a small, curved staircase.

"Is anybody home?" I called out. "May I come up?"

"Who is it, please?" replied a voice from the head of the stairs.

"Gemma Johnstone. If it's not convenient at the moment I
can come back later."

"It's all right. Do come up," replied the old lady, as I knew she
would. Isolated way up here on top of the house, she must be
starved for visitors. I climbed the circular staircase and entered a
time warp, or so it struck me at first glance. Victorian furniture,
dark, massive, mahogany, compressed a space made even smaller
by wallpaper in an exploding pattern of enormous peonies. On
every available flat surface stood rows of photographs in tar-
nished silver frames. Light pouring through three large curved
windows did its best to neutralize the specific gravity of the
furnishings. One third of the circular space had been partitioned
off to make a bathroom. Dominating the bedroom itself stood an
immense sleigh bed in which sat an old lady who could not
possibly have been anybody but Christine Blake's mother. Blood

may well be thicker than water, but bone structure is the dead giveaway.

"Good morning, Mrs. . . .?"

"Chisholm, Helen Chisholm. I suppose you're the new companion?"

"That remains to be seen."

She lowered her voice, making the tone confidential, almost conspiratorial. "I don't suppose you happen to have a cigarette?"

"No, I never smoke."

"Oh, dear," she slumped back against the pillows in an attitude of disappointment, "another one who's worried about her lungs."

"It's not my lungs that concern me, but my skin. Smoking is terrible for the complexion."

"At my age that's hardly a concern. Vanity is for the young. Since my daughter stopped smoking she has turned the entire house into a non-smoking area. I bribed the cook to bring me cigarettes, but Christine found out and threatened to fire the woman."

I took note that a package of cigarettes might well tip the scales in a power struggle. "Now, Mrs. Chisholm, the morning is half gone. Why are you still in bed?"

"Why not? What else do I have to do?"

"What you must do is to sit in a chair and let me do something with your hair." The hair in question, white and still abundant, had been pulled straight back and imprisoned by a red rubber band from which hanks fell to the old lady's shoulders. She wore a bed jacket, a hideously pretty shawl with wide, open sleeves, knitted on giant wooden needles. The pale blue satin bow fastening the garment at the neck looked so bandbox fresh I suspected the jacket had been donned just for the interview.

"What's wrong with my hair?"

"Nothing at all, if you are about to scrub floors or wash windows. Do you have a robe? I don't want you to catch cold."

"In the bathroom."

From the back of the bathroom door I fetched a quilted robe embroidered in food stains. If I had my way it would soon be sloshing around in the washing machine. "Here you are. Do you need a hand?"

"No, I don't, thank you." As if to demonstrate her independence, the old lady threw back the covers and swung her legs over the side of the bed. Pushing her feet into embroidered Chinese slippers, she tugged off the bed jacket and pulled on the robe which I held for her.

"Very good, Mrs. Chisholm. Now sit here, please." I indicated a chair in front of a small dressing table surrounded by a flounce in flowered *cretonne*. The glass top was piled high with magazines, suggesting it was no longer used as a vanity. I moved the periodicals onto the floor. "Now, where are the hairpins, and where is your moisturizer?"

"Hairpins are in the drawer. I don't have any moisturizer."

I spied a bottle of hand lotion on the night table. "Moisten your palms generously with this and massage it carefully into your face. One can't be too careful with one's skin with the central heating turned on."

"Why bother?" Her reflection in the mirror smiled at mine. "I'm still going to look like an alligator handbag."

I smiled back. "Try some. You will be surprised at how much more comfortable your skin will feel." I picked up a large, old fashioned, tortoiseshell comb and began to comb hair which was none too clean. One day soon Mrs. Chisholm and I were going to have a little talk about personal hygiene.

On the other hand, oily hair is easier to dress. In short order I had coaxed the hair, not too severely, back from the old lady's face, now shiny with hand lotion, and folded it neatly into a French roll. I dabbed the excess lotion from her face with Kleenex, then looked in the dressing table drawers for makeup. To my surprise I found everything I needed, lipstick, eyeliner, blush, unopened since the day they had been bought. They were not the shades I would have chosen for her particular skin, which age had turned almost transparent, but I made do.

I am really quite adept at doing hair and applying makeup, having sent more than one admirer, drawn from hangover and puffy from lack of sleep, off to an important meeting looking the picture of health. All it took was a little foundation, a hint of colour, sparingly applied, artfully blended. I am also skilled at cutting men's hair. So many men of a certain age, anxious to prove themselves sexually vigorous, are leery of sensuality. For them the glans is the only erogenous zone. They mistrust hot baths and relaxing massage, preferring cold showers and brisk towelling. Having me cut their hair allows them the pleasure of having their scalp teased and tickled, but all in the service of good grooming. Even when giving pleasure I have so often had to revert to subterfuge.

"Have a look," I said, moving to one side so as not to block the mirror.

"Will you fetch me my glasses, please? They're on the night table."

I crossed to pick up the glasses. She slid them on and turned to her reflection in the mirror. Astonishment made her mute.

Helen Chisholm must once have been a remarkable looking

woman. Even now, with her hair pinned up, a little colour on her mouth and cheeks, she appeared a handsome old lady, aquiline, patrician—light years away from the harridan who had greeted me.

From the moment I entered the room I had been aware of a contrast, a discrepancy between the way Mrs. Chisholm looked and the way she spoke. From a face which would have looked quite at home in *Macbeth*, Act I, Scene I, issued a voice of such mellifluous refinement as to be truly startling. Even the slight huskiness resulting from age and cigarettes could not suppress the beauty of tone and elegance of diction, hovering in that never-never land between Canada and the U.K. It was a pre-television voice, echoing an earlier time when how you spoke helped determine who you were. How could Christine Blake have developed such harsh, hectoring speech with this paragon to hear and emulate?

Mrs. Chisholm continued to study herself in the mirror. Her silence was all the accolade I needed.

I seized the advantage. "Can I assume I have been hired?"

The old lady turned to peer at me suspiciously through tortoiseshell rimmed lenses. "Why are you asking me? Christine does the hiring and firing in this house."

"I told your daughter I would not undertake the job unless I had your approval. I could not possibly spend two weeks in the company of someone who did not want me around."

As if for reassurance, Mrs. Chisholm took a second look at her reflection in the mirror. "Yes, you're hired."

"Very well then, ma'am. I will go and tell Mrs. Blake that you are satisfied. Until next week then." I smiled into the mirror.

As I was just going out the door she spoke. "What do you use on your hair, to get that colour I mean?"

"Nothing."

"Nothing?"

"Nothing at all."

"Extraordinary!" She returned to study her reflection, affirming what I have always believed, that we never grow too old for vanity.

I went down to the third floor. Five bedrooms and a bathroom opened off a central hall. All but one, whose door was shut, appeared to be furnished in Early Salvation Army, a style which develops from putting into each room the basic bedroom components: a bed, a chest of drawers, a chair, a lamp, curtains. For the pure Early Salvation Army look these pieces must be totally mismatched, having neither period, nor colour, nor texture, nor anything else in common. In earlier days this same furniture would have been shipped off to the country house. Today, however, the invasion of white wicker has turned most rural retreats into M.G.M. Malaysia.

A couple of bedrooms showed evidence of once having been inhabited by teenagers: a row of listless dolls propped up on a window seat; a few tired pennants; a couple of posters, curling around the edges, advertising rock concerts. One of the bedroom doors was shut. I opened it, peered briefly at the chaos inside, and closed it quickly. If the cook kept the kitchen the way she maintained her bedroom, I was in for trouble.

I continued down to the ground floor. From the first landing a door opened onto a staircase leading down to the butler's pantry. Steep and narrow, the stairs were faintly lit by one of those low-wattage bulbs favoured by slum landlords and people

who still save string. As I did not wish to set a precedent, and
suggest that I was meekly prepared to use the servants' stairs, I
continued down to the front hall. Mrs. Blake was not in the
living room, nor was she in the den next door, an all-purpose
family room with a large-screen television. I crossed the front
hall into the cheerless dining room, whose long mahogany table
and matching armchairs made it seem less Old Westmount than
Westmount Trust and Loan. I pushed my way through a swinging
door into the butler's pantry, now converted to a bar.

To the right, a door opened into the kitchen, and my first
glimpse of the room caused me to pause in astonishment. Judging
from the rest of the house I would have expected the kitchen to
be old fashioned, or at least traditional, standard appliances in a
mock-colonial setting. Instead I was confronted by a gleaming
expanse of white melamine, formica, tile, all suggesting a clinical
aura more suitable for a lab or a surgery than the focal point of a
household.

Seeing the kitchen explained why the cook wore a white uniform, instead of the more traditional morning green. Her dumpy,
unappetizing presence blocked access to the stove. I could tell by
the way she stirred whatever was in the pot that she hated her job.

"Good morning," I said, a shade too brightly, "I'm looking for
Mrs. Blake."

"She's upstairs," replied the woman without looking up.

"As I will be using the kitchen for two weeks, is there anything you think I should know, about the appliances perhaps?"

The woman stopped stirring long enough to give me a sul-
phurous look, torn between her instinctive dislike for me and a
desire to shaft her employer. Malice triumphed over mistrust.

"If you want my advice, don't take the job. I suppose she told

you I was leavin' to look after my sister. If I told her I was quittin'
she wouldn't give me a decent reference. She's like that, a real—
I shouldn't say it—bitch! Don't take the job."

I smiled one of those all-purpose, disarming, please-don't-
strike-me smiles and withdrew. Mrs. Blake was just coming down
the stairs.

"There you are, Miss Johnstone. You've had your interview
with Mother?"

"Yes, and she has agreed I should look after her while you are
away. When would you like me to begin?"

"We fly to Florida a week from tomorrow. So why don't you
come in on Monday, a week today, that is."

"Very good. I would prefer you to be here on my first day. I am
certain to have questions. And perhaps it would be a good idea
if I took the room next to the stairs. Then I can hear your mother
if she should need me during the night."

"Good idea." The telephone rang in the den. Mrs. Blake
excused herself to answer, and I let myself out.

I was not overwhelmed with enthusiasm at the prospect of my
new job, but in spite of the cook's sibylline utterance I felt I
could survive the next two weeks. One can get through almost
anything if taken one day at a time.

Three

onday morning I awoke early, my eyes flying open like those of a Sleepy Time Jane doll held upright. I felt the same surge of energy as though I were about to leave for the airport or train station, beckoned by a distant destination which might well turn out to be unfriendly. I ran through the exercises I do every morning when I wake up alone, as I prefer to count on muscle tone rather than foundation garments to make a dress hang properly.

For my first day on the job I scrupulously avoided wearing colour, restricting myself to a plain gray skirt and a gray cardigan over the same Peter Pan blouse I had worn to the interview. At the neck of the blouse I pinned a large cameo, handsome I suppose, although I had never worn it before. It was a gift from an Italian admirer who gave me any amount of real jewellery, "real" in his case meaning organic rather than mineral. Along with the cameo, a carved bit of shell, he gave me a pink coral necklace whose tiny arms and protuberances reminded me of a lethal bacillus greatly magnified. He also presented me with a string of amber beads, great lumps of homemade toffee. Fortunately, there were no bugs trapped in the centre. Unfortunately, you have to be a fortune teller or a piano teacher to wear amber. Even if I liked ivory I wouldn't dare wear the bracelet he handed me on my birthday, although it happened before animal rights became more fashionable than ivory accessories. The only organic jewellery I really fancy is pearls, but there were budgetary limits to his devotion.

I knew that if I took the bus up to Buckingham Gardens I would feel like a charwoman, so I took a taxi. Walking up to the front door with only a little less trepidation than I had the first time, I rang the bell and waited.

And waited. Finally the door flew open in a rush of air. "Oh, it's you, Miss Johnstone," said Christine Blake as though greeting the plumber. She clutched the neck of her old rose housecoat with one hand. "I left the side door to the kitchen open for you."

"Sorry, I didn't know. I should have thought to take a key."

"A key?" she repeated, as though I had just asked for a handout.

"I'm going to need one while you're away, unless you want me to leave the house unlocked when I go out."

"Of course you must have one." By now we were in the front hall. "You must excuse me," she said. "I have a million things to do."

"At your convenience I would like fifteen minutes of your time. I have a list of questions about general maintenance."

"Very good. Why don't you go and deal with Mother, and I'll speak to you later."

I hung up my coat and climbed to the tower room. Mrs. Chisholm sat in bed reading, a mug of coffee at her elbow. Today she had not made the slightest attempt at grooming. Over a shapeless cardigan her hair hung down in two loose braids: Heidi in her dotage.

"Good morning, Mrs. Chisholm."

"Good morning, Gemma. You're bright and early, I'm glad to see."

"Have you had breakfast?"

"Oh, I never eat it."

"Is that because you don't like breakfast, or because nobody bothers to serve you a decent one?"

My question surprised her. She put down her book and took off her glasses, the better to see me at a distance.

"Will you at least try my excellent scrambled eggs?" I asked before she could reply.

"That might be very pleasant for a change."

I returned to the kitchen where the table, a slab of mellow pine, installed I suspect to soften the otherwise clinical room, was still littered with the fallout from a Spartan breakfast. Opening cupboards and drawers, I unearthed a mixing bowl and a skillet. In a refrigerator crammed with jars covered in aluminum foil I found eggs and a block of cheddar.

I scrambled two eggs, adding a dash of water while beating them before folding in a little grated cheddar and a few drops of Worcestershire sauce. Cook them slowly over slow heat, stirring gently until just firm, and you have scrambled eggs fit for an earl. Only my Eggs Benedict are fit for a king.

I placed the eggs on a slice of buttered toast, as I knew by the time I carried the tray upstairs that regular toast would be cold.

One tentative bite was all it took before Mrs. Chisholm tucked in and cleaned her plate, washing it down with a cup of fresh coffee I had brewed. It did not take a fertile imagination to picture the cold toast and rubbery eggs that slatternly cook would have served.

"Delicious, quite delicious," was her comment. "I can't remember the last time I ate breakfast."

"And now it's time for your bath," I said as I removed the tray. "Do you need help getting in and out of the tub?"

"Not really. But I had a bath yesterday."

"Your hair will be easier to do if it's clean," I fibbed, anxious to see it washed.

"I have trouble shampooing it in the tub."

I was struck by a sudden idea. "Mrs. Chisholm, did I not see a shower in the bathroom one floor down?"

"Yes, why?"

"It's much easier to wash your hair under running water than in the tub."

The old lady gave me a look of astonishment tinged with alarm. "I can't take stairs."

"Why not?"

"My legs. I'm all right going down, but I can't get back up. I have to be carried."

"When did you last try?" I continued relentlessly. "Watching you get out of that bed leaves me in no doubt that you can manage stairs. And if you can't, we will have you carried back up. You simply cannot spend your life cooped up in this tower room."

"Christine doesn't want me to risk going downstairs. She's afraid I may fall and break something. Then it will be a hospital and a nursing home, or so she says. And I don't want to move. This is my house. And I want to be buried from it."

"I see. Am I to understand that you own this house, that 27 Buckingham Gardens is your property?"

"Yes."

"And with all the rooms this house must have, you are kept up here?" I was on the point of adding, "like the mad Mrs. Rochester in *Jane Eyre*," but I wanted to appear casual, not tendentious.

"Yes, Christine says this way I won't be disturbed. But the problem is that I'd love to be disturbed. I never get to see anyone."

"Well, I'm here to take care of that. Now, answer me honestly. Is there anything seriously wrong with your legs, other than the usual encroachments of old age?"

"Not really."

I reached out and took one of her hands in mine. There are moments—don't I know—when touch can be far more eloquent than speech. "Then if I took your arm firmly and you gripped the bannister with your free hand, is there any real reason you could not take the stairs?"

"I don't think so."

"If we run into difficulties we will simply install you comfortably and call for porters to carry you back up. Shall we go?"

I could see the old lady torn between conflicting impulses. The first was to maintain the *status quo*, to remain safely in her tower room. But although we may outgrow a taste for cookies, we never really lose the urge to raid the cookie jar.

"Why not?" she said as she rose to her feet. "'In for a penny, in for a pound.'"

"'It's love that makes the world go round.'" I concluded.

We both started to laugh. At that moment I knew I had made a breakthrough.

I was right of course. Mrs. Chisholm turned out to be more steady on her legs than she had suspected, and we made our way down to the third floor without mishap. I got the shower running, then waited outside the bathroom until she was installed behind the frosted glass door. A nurse is used to seeing all kinds and shapes of people in every stage of dress or undress. Mrs. Chisholm's bare body held no terrors for me. But I wanted to spare her the embarrassment of standing naked in my presence, of exposing her shrunken body to the gaze of a stranger. This way, concealed behind the distorting glass, she could maintain the illusion of modesty, even as I handed the shampoo bottle over the top of the door.

I waited outside the bathroom until she had dried herself and pulled on the clean nightdress I had brought down from her room. Then I was able to help her back into her robe and wrap a towel, turban style, around her wet hair. With her left arm tucked securely under my right, her own right hand gripping the stair rail, we took the steps one at a time back to the tower room.

After settling her in an arm chair, I towelled her hair as dry as I could before combing it out loose. I handed her the book and her glasses, and straightened up the bed.

"If you are all right for a moment, Mrs. Chisholm, I would like to speak to your daughter."

"I'll be fine." She gave me a reluctant smile. "I had forgotten how good it feels to take a shower."

"I never take anything but a shower." I returned the smile. We now had a shared enthusiasm and I went downstairs feeling that the next two weeks might not be so bad after all.

Mrs. Blake was nowhere to be found; the house appeared to be empty except for Mrs. Chisholm and myself. I decided to make use of the time to familiarize myself with the kitchen, to the casual eye a room designed for efficiency. Reaching for the gleaming chrome handle on a spotless melamine cupboard door opening on noiseless hinges, I studied the chaos within, only to be reminded of a radio program I had listened to as a girl, seated in front of the art deco radio shaped like a gothic arch. The program was *Fibber McGee and Molly*. At least once during the program, in spite of Molly's dire warnings, Fibber McGee would open the closet door. All hell broke loose as objects, held in place only by the closed door, cascaded onto the floor.

The Blake household cupboards did not discharge their contents when opened, but they lacked any kind of organizing principle. I could tell by the way things were jammed haphazardly onto shelves that the cook was incompetent. In order to reach anything at all it was necessary to move something else. Condiments crouched behind measuring cups and graters. Mixing bowls served as catchalls for everything from rubber bands to discount coupons. The meagre array of spices had been banished to the back of the shelf, their labels impossible to read without lifting them out one by one.

Drawers slid out on silent runners to display chrome utensils with rust bleeding through their finish beside spatulas whose edges had been fluted by heat from the dishwasher. State-of-the-art drawer dividers held blunt paring knives, charred wooden spoons, scratched plastic scrapers, all looking as though they had been bought at a down-market rummage sale.

While making Mrs. Chisholm's breakfast I had noticed the large refrigerator filled with what I took to be leftovers. Now, I reached at random for a jar and removed the foil to discover mold so luxuriant that I flushed the contents down the toilet, conveniently located beside the coatroom. A jar of marmalade so antique the sugar had crystallized went into the trash, followed by a bottle of salad dressing whose ingredients had separated. I suppose I could be called presumptuous, going into someone else's refrigerator and throwing out their leftovers. However, gone-by food is not only unpleasant; it is a hazard. Disorganization and clutter quickly gave way to order and space.

There is something at once soothing and satisfying about a good cleaning. The beneficial effects show almost at once. I have always been orderly, even as a child. In spite of the psychological cant about early toilet training and confinement in playpens, I have always suspected certain children develop habits of compulsive neatness as a defense against the disorder in which they inexplicably find themselves. Such was certainly the case with me.

My father had been a violent man, even with Mother. Demonstrating not a little pluck, she left him, at a time when most women meekly accepted that they had married for better or for worse, and resigned themselves to the worse.

Father mistrusted banks; as a result he kept his money in a strongbox in the bottom drawer of his rolltop desk. A badly bruised Mother pinched the key one night while he was sleeping off a bender. She and I, each carrying a single suitcase, rode the train from Birmingham to Liverpool where she bought two tickets to Montreal on the *Empress of Canada*.

As all the less expensive tourist cabins had long been booked, we were obliged to travel first class. I was only thirteen when we sailed down the Mersey into open water, but I am convinced it was that first taste of gracious living which altered the course of my life. After a childhood of post-wartime austerity—food rationing, hand-me-down clothing, making do and going without—I found myself quite dazzled by the cornucopia provided by Canada Steamships. I could scarcely believe there was meat on the menu at every meal. Hot water poured in endless streams from taps, to be blotted up by stacks of towels replenished at least twice daily.

Consommé and crackers at eleven, tea and cakes at four, sandwiches in the stateroom at bedtime, and nobody to say, "Stop! You've had your share." It certainly beat bubble and squeak, toad-in-the-hole, bangers and mash, plaice and chips, plums and custard.

Mother fretted about the money it had cost. Cursed with the adult awareness that out there crouched the future, she worried about arriving penniless in the New World. Not I. Surrounded as we were by that vast gray expanse of Atlantic Ocean, stretching unbroken to nudge the horizon, I believed the voyage would not, could not, end. It was the sight of that great ship pulled and pushed by grimy tugs up to a Montreal pier that caused the first tears since we had left Birmingham.

We did not arrive quite so penniless as Mother had initially feared. During the last days of the crossing, Mother had insisted I go to the afternoon movie so she could take a rest. She was most emphatic about not being disturbed. Mother never looked particularly rested after these naps, and the cabin often had a faint smell of cigar smoke. At the time I drew no conclusions.

If I did not think it odd that Mother's fatigue obliged me to sit through the same movie twice or, on occasion, to dine alone at a table crackling with starched linen while she had something on a tray in the stateroom, it was because I had been making a few discoveries of my own. Although not yet fourteen and dressed in a hideously jejune fashion, all puffed sleeves and flounces and eyelet trim, I still had something that drew men. They sidled up to me on the promenade deck and stood closer than was necessary to be heard above the wind. They put their hands on my knee at the movies and asked if I was enjoying the film. They put their arms affectionately around my shoulders and accidentally brushed my breasts, which had begun to swell proudly. They asked me to dance, their wives smiling approval at the kindly, avuncular gesture, then pushed their thing hard against my abdomen. They offered to buy me drinks, ginger ale when the wives were present, champagne cocktails when they were not. And they were pleasant, cloyingly pleasant, aggressively, overpoweringly pleasant, as they playfully took my hand, or touched my pretty hair, or tried to look down the front of my dress. And I understood I had power, even though I did not yet know how to wield it.

By the time we walked down the gangplank in Montreal, Mother had enough cash for a month's rent on a seedy apartment and the down payment on a sewing machine. She set herself up as a seamstress specializing in alterations. Between bouts of stitching she also managed a little hooking, as I learned one afternoon when I came home early from school and found her in bed with the landlord.

I once asked Mother why she had saddled me with a name like Gemma. Was it because it incorporated her own name, Emma?

"Not really," Mother had replied. "I was seriously considering Lettice or Yvonne, but I thought Gemma prettier."

Given the alternatives I had to admit I came out ahead.

Four

The side door opened to admit Christine Blake carrying a bag of groceries, which she put down on the counter. I shut the door.

"I'm glad you're back, Mrs. Blake. Not surprisingly, I have some questions."

Without looking up she began to unpack. "Yes?"

"Is your mother taking any medication?"

"Not at the moment. She has nitroglycerine tablets in the night table in case she has an attack of angina. But since I persuaded her to give up smoking, her heart has been behaving itself quite nicely."

"Very good. Now I would like the name and number of her doctor and her pharmacist, along with the names and numbers of those companies that service the house: the plumber, the electrician, whoever repairs the furnace—anyone I might need to call while you are away."

"I'll make up a list." Sliding a chunk of beef from a plastic bag she gave a small gasp of impatience. "Damn!" she muttered. "Blade steak! Whatever was I thinking?"

I rose and crossed to the counter. "Is that tonight's dinner?"

"Yes, I was going to do it under the grill."

"It's too fat to grill properly. But it could be managed in a slow oven. Do you have any red cooking wine?"

"I think so."

"Good. If you can find me some onions, consommé or beef broth, bay leaf, and capers, I can do something with the beef before I leave this afternoon. Oh, and I'll need a flat casserole. Just leave things on the counter. Now I'd better go and see if your mother is ready for her lunch."

I pushed my way through the swinging door into the dining room and went up to the second floor. The door to the bedroom at the head of the stairs stood ajar, and prompted by curiosity, I stepped inside. A large room, drenched in light, it was dominated by a handsome fireplace faced in iridescent pink tiles. To the left of the fireplace a door opened onto a covered balcony. Being on the rear of the house, the windows commanded a superb view over the city to the St. Lawrence River. On a clear day it would almost be possible to see Vermont.

The room had been furnished in Danish teak, once in the forefront of contemporary design and now almost as traditional as colonial pine. Still, the mellow wood made the room warm and inviting, as did the woven bedspread and curtains. I suspected the room had been done by a professional decorator.

In the far corner a door opened into a large bathroom equipped with beautiful old porcelain fixtures. A tapered pedestal supported the sink, while the tub sat on four elegant claw and ball feet. So generous was the space it had been possible to install a shower stall in one corner without interfering with the existing fixtures.

The only personal touch in the bedroom was a studio portrait in an ornate silver frame which, on closer inspection, turned out to be Mrs. Chisholm wearing a small fitted hat and a silver fox neckpiece. Her elegant neck arched gracefully as she gazed not quite into the camera, apparently oblivious to the confusion of clamped jaws, glass eyes, tiny paws, and bushy tails swarming around her shoulders. Animal rights aside, the wearing of whole pelts around the neck had to be one of the uglier fashions ever visited upon women, not to mention the fact that the only creature who should wear a silver fox pelt is a silver fox.

As Mrs. Chisholm was not in the habit of eating breakfast, she found her appetite still stunned by the scrambled eggs. But she seemed receptive to my suggestion of salad and a pot of tea. By now her hair had dried and was twisted into two loose plaits which made her look like someone who has just woven a shawl on a hand loom. When she became a bit more used to me I would suggest having it cut; but "Rome wasn't built in a day," as the late lamented Walter used to say. Neither were Montreal, London, or Moscow; but perhaps being dubbed "The Eternal City" has caused unfortunate Rome to be trapped in that tired platitude.

Downstairs in the kitchen, in what is laughingly called the crisper, I found a head of tired lettuce which made me think of Cinderella at one a.m. By dint of rummaging around I was able to improvise a chef's salad: lettuce, tinned tuna, a couple of hard-boiled eggs, grated cheddar, all tossed with a vinaigrette made, unfortunately, with corn oil. A kitchen without olive oil is like sunshine without a day.

I made lunch for two and carried the tray upstairs. At first Mrs. Chisholm seemed leery of my sharing lunch with her, but whether it was me personally or simply that she was accustomed to eating alone, I couldn't tell. I wasn't exactly help, nor was I her social equal. I moved in limbo; to all outward appearances a lady, but in the subservient position of waiting on her to earn my salary, a subject which still had to be settled.

I became businesslike, and in short order learned the name of her doctor. I also learned the name and number of the electrician were posted beside the circuit breakers, that of the plumber on the hot water tank, and the service number for the furnace on a nearby wall.

"You seem to be very knowledgeable about home maintenance," I said as I poured tea.

"It was, *is* my house, as I think I told you. I ran it for years. I still pay for the upkeep—taxes, insurance, maintenance—only Christine writes the cheques."

"Does she have power of attorney?"

"Yes, she does. Last fall I had a bad bout of pneumonia. I don't have to tell you that for an older person it can be a serious illness. It was touch and go for a while. While I was recuperating, Christine and the doctor persuaded me that granting her power of attorney would be best for all concerned. I was too depleted to argue, so I signed.

"I couldn't smoke when I was ill, and once I recovered, Christine got the doctor's approval to deny me cigarettes. I've always had a tricky heart, and now smoking has joined the lengthening list of activities to avoid. Wasn't it Wordsworth who said, 'The child is father to the man'? Well, Christine seized the opportunity to become the mother to the woman and forbade cigarettes in the house. She had just stopped smoking herself and saw God in an empty ashtray, the Devil in a lighted match."

I was amused by the conceit, but kept myself from laughing. The less one draws attention to oneself, the more one is likely to learn. "Was it after your illness that you moved into this upstairs room?" I asked, as casually as if I had been inquiring the time.

"Correct. It was Christine's idea to put me up here. She claimed I wouldn't be disturbed by the comings and goings in the house.

Her rationale was that the less I was exposed to stress, the better it would be for my heart." The old lady gave a sharp laugh, more like a cough. "She was right. Nothing disturbs me. I never get to see anybody, only Christine when she brings me coffee in the morning and the cook serving me meals."

I continued to poke at my salad, which was not too bad, considering. "Now that you are so obviously recovered, why don't you move back downstairs?"

Mrs. Chisholm paused before answering. "I'd love to. My room was the one right at the head of the stairs; it has a beautiful fireplace. But Christine had the room redecorated, and now it is used as a guest room."

I kept my voice studiously neutral. "But it is your house, after all. More tea?"

"Yes, thank you. And you're right; it is my house. But I'm an old lady, Gemma. I can no longer function by myself. My son is divorced and lives in a condominium in Toronto. Without Christine I would have to move into what is euphemistically called a senior citizens' residence, read old people's home."

"There are worse places," I suggested. Then leaning forward, I spoke with a kind of calculated, slightly breathless enthusiasm, pitching my voice higher than normal to simulate girlishness. "Mrs. Chisholm, I'd like you to think about something. Don't say yes or no, but just listen. Tomorrow, after your daughter leaves for her cruise, why don't you move downstairs to your old room, if only for the two weeks she will be away. That means you could come downstairs for meals; we could watch TV in the den. I will be able to look after you better," I added in my best propaganda voice, carefully skirting any suggestion of self-interest. (Who wouldn't want to save herself two flights of stairs?) "Anytime you might want a cup of tea, or an orange say, or a fresh package of cigarettes . . ."

Mrs. Chisholm snapped to attention. "Cigarettes! Did you say cigarettes?"

"I may not smoke them, but I am certainly old enough to buy them." Having played my trump card, I changed the subject. "Do you generally have a nap after lunch?"

"As a rule."

"Let me get you settled."

After seeing her safely stowed in bed, her book and glasses within reach, I picked up the lunch tray.

"You really did say cigarettes?" she asked.

"Yes. Did you smoke a particular brand?"

"Not really, just so long as it's tobacco. And none of those prissy filter tips!"

I nodded my complicity and went out. On my way down the stairs I met Mrs. Blake, who announced she was off to have her hair done. She looked frayed; anxious creases bracketed her mouth. Travel is never as much fun as the ads suggest.

I went into the kitchen and started the dishwasher. My fingers almost twitched with the urge to reorganize, but I decided it would be more prudent to wait until Mrs. Blake had left. I read the paper, then made tea for Mrs. Chisholm, who was just climbing out of sleep as I entered her room. I left her watching a rerun of *Sesame Street*—the letter "M" was being given star billing—and returned to the kitchen to deal with the blade steak.

Christine Blake had either neglected or forgotten to put out the ingredients I had requested for making dinner, but by now I had enough idea of where things were kept to find what I need-ed, including a clean apron. The chopping board felt sticky and had to be scrubbed.

In minutes I had seared the beef which I put into a shallow casserole with red wine, beef stock and capers. After tucking bay leaves around the edges of the meat I slid the casserole into an oven preset to 350° Fahrenheit.

The side door opened and a man came into the kitchen. His evident surprise at seeing me made him pause just a moment before saying, "Good evening."

"Good evening, sir. Are you Mr. Blake?"

"In a manner of speaking," he replied and smiled, causing the corners of his eyes to wrinkle winsomely. I suspected a ready smile was part of his protective colouring, like the stripes on a tiger which cause him to disappear in the long grass. "Are you the new cook?"

"No, sir. I have been engaged to look after Mrs. Chisholm for the next two weeks. I'm just getting dinner underway. Mrs. Blake is at the hairdresser."

"Naturally." He crossed into the butler's pantry, put down his briefcase, and poured himself a drink which looked like a dry martini on the rocks. Instead of going into the main part of the house, he came to lounge in the kitchen door, leaning his weight against the door frame.

"What's your name?"

"Gemma Johnstone."

"I'm Arthur Morris. Cheers, Gemma." He drank. It did not escape my notice that he had moved at once onto a first name basis. Accustomed as I am to sizing up men, I could tell he relied heavily on his charm; one could almost have said boyish charm, but Arthur Morris was no longer a boy. Lines around the eyes, usually a pretty good indicator of age, hinted at forty-five plus, although his tall, lean figure and thick auburn hair, only flecked with gray, made him appear younger. The youthful look was enhanced by expensively tailored preppy clothes, the tweed jacket, button-down blue oxford shirt, striped tie, chinos, and loafers which were the Ivy League uniform of the Fifties.

I also understood he was checking me out. Those for whom sexuality is a focus develop an instinct about others. To use an inelegant expression, Arthur Morris was sniffing around, trying to learn whether I would be complaisant were he to exercise his *droit du seigneur*. But, to paraphrase another vulgar saw, I do not defecate where I feed.

"Tastes good," he said, winking at his drink and, by extension, at me. "I had to keep office hours today."

"You teach at the university, Mr. Morris?"

"Yes, and please call me Arthur."

I smiled vaguely. Under no circumstances was I going to get onto a first name basis with the man of the household, especially while working for his wife and mother-in-law.

"I'm on sabbatical this year," he continued. "That's why I am able to go on this cruise. But I have a couple of students writing theses under my supervision, and they wanted to see me before I left. Will you be staying on after we get back?"

"That remains to be seen."

Christine Blake came in through the side door as if entering Government House. "Oh, you're home, Arthur. I don't suppose that's mineral water in your glass. I see you've met Miss Johnstone."

"We introduced ourselves." He flashed one last winning grin before pushing through the swinging door into the house.

"I just put the beef into the oven, Mrs. Blake. Leave it at 350 for an hour or so, then turn the heat down to 300. After two, maybe two-and-a-half hours it should be ready to serve, with noodles or rice. I prefer noodles myself."

"That's awfully good of you," she replied in a voice which, if I had hackles, would have caused them to rise. It is a vocal trick the rich have down pat, thanking you for something you know perfectly well they have taken for granted. "And now I must go and finish packing. Will you be here in time to serve Mother her breakfast tomorrow?"

"If you like. Half past eight?"

"That will be fine. Goodnight then."

She strode from the kitchen, having dismissed me. For one rebellious moment I was tempted to follow her upstairs, demand a house key, insist on determining my salary, and learn what I was to do about petty cash for household expenses. However, I suspected that Christine Blake thrived on confrontation, and I had my own more subtle weapons. Still, it struck me as odd that she would take off for two weeks, leaving a woman she had only just met in charge of both her mother and her house. But I have often observed that the rich are careless. They can afford to be, secure in the knowledge that a solid bank account makes a substantial buffer against the inconveniences of daily life.

Given the opportunity for a cruise, I might have left my house—but certainly not my mother—in the charge of a stranger. However, I was already beginning to suspect there was no love lost between Mrs. Chisholm and her daughter. Far from feeling regret for having taken on the job, I could hardly wait for tomorrow's instalment of "Gemma Johnstone: Girl Companion," a *roman à clef* with the key left under the mat.

Five

uesday morning, dressed as modestly as a social worker, I went to the side door of 27 Buckingham Gardens, only to find it locked. Retracing my steps around to the front, I rang the bell and resigned myself to a long wait. After a while, Mrs. Blake opened the door. She wore the expression of a nun who has just watched a man expose himself.

"Sorry to keep bothering you, Mrs. Blake, but I still don't have a key."

"I'll leave one on the kitchen table," she tossed over her shoulder as she headed up the stairs.

The door to the living room was almost blocked by a pyramid of luggage. One would have thought Christine Blake and husband were heading around the world. I hung up my coat and carried my suitcase up to the third floor before checking in on Mrs. Chisholm.

"Thank goodness you're here," she grumbled. "I haven't had my coffee yet."

"On the double."

I went down to the kitchen to find Arthur Morris in a handsome velour robe reading the paper. Looking up, he beamed his winsome smile as I poured coffee. "What time do you leave?" I asked.

"Around ten, or whenever Christine gets it together." He glanced at the clock. "Time to shower." He stood, giving me an opportunity to see his legs, which were long and sexy.

Upstairs, Mrs. Chisholm slurped greedily at her coffee. Casually I drew a package of Camels from the pocket of my skirt. "Would you care for one of these? You won't even have to walk a mile."

"Would I!" In her eagerness she almost spilled the coffee.

"First you must get out of bed and sit in a chair. I have one injunction regarding smoking, only one: you must never smoke in bed. I am certain I am breaking house rules to accommodate you, and in turn you must cooperate with me. Are we agreed?"

"Agreed." With astonishing agility Mrs. Chisholm scrambled out of bed and into her robe. While she settled herself in the armchair, a small brass bowl in her lap to serve as ashtray, I opened the package, teased out a cigarette, and struck a match. Mrs. Chisholm inhaled so deeply I would not have been surprised to see smoke pouring from her slippers. She closed her eyes in rapture, then slowly let the smoke escape. I stood sentinel at the door in case Mrs. Blake should burst in unexpectedly.

"Not being a smoker you have no idea how good that tastes." She inhaled again.

"I am probably shortening my life with every puff, but a cigarette is one of the few things left which can still make me feel fully alive. I'm prepared to take my chances." It did not take her long to smoke the cigarette right down to her fingers, so close in fact, I feared she might scorch the skin.

I flushed the evidence down the toilet and gave the room a couple of blasts of air freshener to cover the smell of smoke. Mrs. Chisholm insisted she wanted no breakfast, but her resistance crumpled at the promise of another cigarette. A few packs of Camels and I could call the shots. It seemed like a pretty good trade-off.

I tidied up the kitchen and made Mrs. Chisholm French toast, fried a light golden-brown, the colour of autumn leaves. I sprinkled it lightly with demerara sugar. There was a tin of maple syrup in the refrigerator, which looked as if it had been bought for Expo '67. It is a vile liquid, with an unpleasant aftertaste to the intense sweetness, much beloved by those for whom frosting a cake is the *ne plus ultra* of culinary skill.

I sat with Mrs. Chisholm while she ate and then smoked another cigarette. No sooner had I flushed the butt and ashes away than Mrs. Blake lunged through the doorway to say good-bye. Her heliotrope suit swelled to fill the entire room. "We're off, Mother, just as soon as the limousine arrives." She bent down to give her mother one of those no-contact kisses. "I'm sure Miss Johnstone will take good care of you while we are gone."

"Well, well, dear. I hope you and Arthur have a second honeymoon."

"I'd be happy to settle for a first." Mrs. Blake paused for a moment and gave a suspicious sniff. "I'll send you postcards from our various ports of call, for all the good it will do. We'll be back weeks before the cards arrive. Ta-ta. Miss Johnstone, a word."

I followed the daughter from the room and down to the second floor, where she turned to confront me.

"I've left a key on the kitchen table. It works on all the doors. I also left an envelope with housekeeping money. Should anything unforeseen happen, call my brother in Toronto. Brian Chisholm on Avenue Road. And, Miss Johnstone, under no circumstances are you to let Mother smoke. Is that quite clear?"

I could see that Christine Blake was a bully. With her height and her voice and her undeniable presence she had been endowed with the power to intimidate. Like the talent to please, the ability to browbeat is not given to everyone. However, to remain civil when confronted by a bully does not mean that one has been cowed.

"Very good, Mrs. Blake," I replied mildly. "Do you need a hand with the luggage?"

"No. Arthur and the driver will manage."

I followed her kick pleat down to the front hall. Arthur Morris, a coffee and caramel photo spread from *Gentlemen's Quarterly*, stood with a trench coat draped over his shoulders.

"Is the limousine here yet?" demanded his wife.

"No. What time did you order it for?"

"How should I know? You're the one who was to order the car."

"What do you mean, 'I was to order the car?' You told me, many, many times, that you were taking care of all the arrangements so there would be no hitches." He shrugged the coat from his shoulders.

"Quite right. But I distinctly told you to order the limousine, a large one, to carry the luggage."

"Well, I didn't."

"You mean to say we have no way of getting to the airport?"

I could see a crisis brewing. "Why don't I order you two cabs? You can each go in one and split the luggage."

The soundness of my suggestion could not be faulted, but I suspected Christine Blake would almost have preferred making an issue to being on time for her flight. By the time I ordered the taxis and returned to the front hall the adversaries had retreated into simmering silence. I went to stand sentinel at the living room window.

"Here they come," I called out gaily. I wanted them out of the house so badly I could taste it. As the cabs drove off, Arthur Morris turned to wave goodbye, but Christine Blake was so busy instructing the driver that she moved off without even a backward glance at the house. Happiness was seeing those two taxis disappearing down the crescent and out of sight. It was only then I realized the question of my salary remained unsettled.

The house key lay on an envelope filled with money. I counted the bills onto the kitchen table: one hundred dollars. Hardly enough to run a house this size for two weeks.

I climbed to the tower room. "They're on their way," I announced cheerfully.

"Good! Now I would like to move downstairs."

"You've decided to follow my suggestion?"

"Yes, but I think I'll have one last goodbye cigarette, if I may."

"Mrs. Chisholm," I began as I lit the cigarette, "before you granted your daughter the power of attorney, how did you and she manage household expenses?" I went to stand behind her so I could coil her hair to pin into a soft figure eight.

"We had a joint account. The bulk of the deposits were mine, but we could both write cheques."

"When you granted your daughter the power of attorney, did you, or she, close that account?"

"I don't think so. But now she writes all the cheques."

"I ask because she has left me only one hundred dollars in housekeeping money."

Mrs. Chisholm exhaled sharply. "She's a fool! That isn't even enough to pay the cleaning woman."

"Could you write me a cheque on the household account,

when we run short of funds?"

"I don't see why not. And don't forget; we have several charge accounts." She butted her cigarette. "And now, my dear, I'm ready to move."

By the time Christine Blake and Arthur Morris were airborne, Mrs. Chisholm was comfortably installed in her former bedroom, puffing contentedly on a cigarette, while I carried her personal effects downstairs. By the time she was ready for some lunch, the room looked as though she had been living there for months.

When I stopped to buy cigarettes on my way home the previous night I had taken the precaution of buying Mrs. Chisholm's lunch: paté, brie, a beautiful piece of Stilton, a couple of *baguettes*. I also bought a small ledger in which to record expenditures.

Mrs. Chisholm could not have been more delighted with the fare, which we shared in front of the pink fireplace. "This is a treat, Gemma," her voice caressed the words. "I am awfully sick of tinned soup and a flat sandwich for lunch. I'm so glad the cook has quit. Her meals were dreadful, like hospital food."

"No longer. I am in charge now. What would you like for dinner?"

"Just like that? I can choose a menu?"

"Why not? While you're napping I'll telephone an order."

"It's too late for today. Bradford's will only accept orders for delivery until one o'clock, for the same day that is."

"I'll have them send up the food in a taxi—with your approval naturally."

"What a good idea. Why didn't I think of that?"

"This is probably a two car household. People who drive their own cars think of taxis as instruments of the Devil."

Mrs. Chisholm laughed out loud. "I suppose you're right. I

always felt uncomfortable taking a taxi when I drove my own car. I thought it a terrible waste of money."

"That's because you had to pay cash. People with money hate to part with cash. They will write cheques for huge amounts or produce a credit card without a second thought. But to part with two twenties and a ten is like peeling off a layer of skin."

Mrs. Chisholm laughed again. "I guess I have to agree. Silly, isn't it? Could I have a cigarette, please?"

While she smoked I unpinned her hair in preparation for her nap. "Mrs. Chisholm, have you ever thought of having your hair cut? Not just hacked short, but properly cut and styled. It would be much easier to wash and care for."

"You're quite right. I'd love to wear it short. A woman of my age doesn't have much use for her crowning glory, as we used to call it. The problem is getting to a hairdresser when it is so difficult for me to leave the house."

"What if I knew a hairdresser who is prepared to make house calls?"

"Do you suppose he'd be willing to come all the way up here to Buckingham Gardens?" she asked as she tapped ash from her cigarette.

"He would, if we paid his cab fare."

"Well, if you think you can arrange it . . ."

"I'll see what I can do."

After settling Mrs. Chisholm for her nap I went down to the kitchen and telephoned an order. The butcher assured me the beef could be cut with a fork. The store also carried new potatoes and frozen fiddleheads. I added a few things at random: a large bottle of Spanish olive oil, English biscuits, Japanese rice crackers, Italian pasta. I considered the fiddleheads my patriotic purchase.

I then called Tresses and Tonsure, or T^2 as displayed on the logo, a hairdressing establishment catering to both sexes, and asked to speak to Gino—Gerry to his friends. I never let anyone but Gerry touch my hair. He understands that when I am having my hair done for a big evening, the coiffure must always appear casual, as though it could be let down in seconds. How many men have sought solace in my bed because of their wives' hair, lacquered into helmets which forbid the damaging exertions of sex. Girls today spend money to make their hair look as though they've just rolled out of bed, but I'm a bit mature to be permanently tousled. What's good for the gosling is not necessarily good for the goose.

I explained the situation to Gerry over the phone, and as a favour to me he agreed to come up after his last appointment. I have yet to meet a gay man who won't go out of his way to do me a favour without necessarily expecting one in return. It is the so-called straight men who keep accounts, financial and emotional, with a separate column for interest.

I went back upstairs. Mrs. Chisholm slept, and I took the opportunity to explore the second floor. A small room beside the master bedroom must once have served as dressing room, and almost foundered under the weight of flounces and floral patterns. I decided it would be a good idea for me to sleep there in case Mrs. Chisholm wanted me during the night.

The remaining part of the floor had been turned into a suite, to which the door had been closed. Curiosity drove me to open it and go inside. At the far end of the passageway stood a bathroom, gutted and ruthlessly modernized. Slabs of marble and sheets of formica held the fixtures captive. To the left lay a large bedroom, to the right a smaller one which must have been intended as a dressing room. A king-sized bed dominated the space, not surprising as both Arthur and Christine were tall. What struck me on closer inspection was the profusion of cats. Every surface bristled with figurines, china cats, brass cats, pottery cats, felines in bronze, glass, *cloisonné*. Merely to keep them dusted must be a part-time job. Over the fireplace hung a reproduction of a charming Japanese cat, a large multicoloured bow around its neck, watching an unsuspecting spider from behind a screen. Cross-stitched cats decorated throw pillows, stencilled cats dotted the dresser, cast iron cats did double duty as andirons. The Egyptian cat goddess sat sentinel on the desk, needlepoint cats flanked the mirror, a calico cat hooked into a rug covered the hearth. The cumulative effect was overpowering, obsessive. I have no objection to figurines, but this collection took on the dimensions of an infestation.

I crossed into the smaller room, which bore a decidedly masculine stamp, two mahogany chests and a silent valet supporting a houndstooth suit. Along one wall sat a studio bed, which was made up under the paisley spread, suggesting that Arthur Morris no longer shared the one in the master bedroom. Separate beds may suggest that passion has cooled, but separate rooms, especially when the husband is younger, hint at problems.

I left as silently as I had entered and went down to plug in the kettle for tea. Mrs. Chisholm was just floating up to consciousness when I carried the tray upstairs.

"Mrs. Chisholm," I began, once I had her settled with tea and a cigarette, "I find it odd that in a house this size, moreover one that lies so close to a park, there are no pets. I took for granted there would be a large dog, or at least cats."

"We did have a dog, a German Shepherd, which had belonged to Christine's first husband, Charles Blake. As you may have figured out, Arthur is her second husband. The dog turned out to be furiously jealous of Arthur, snarling and baring its teeth whenever he came into the room." She gave a low chuckle. "Sometimes I think the dog showed excellent judgement, but we had to get rid of him; Christine sent him out to a farm somewhere. She adores cats, but Arthur is terribly allergic to cat hair. I can't say I'm sorry. I dislike small animals underfoot."

The doorbell rang. I went down to find Gerry on the stoop.

"Gorgeous one!" He struck an attitude, hand on hip. "It may be humble, but it's home. I haven't been in this part of town since I stopped cruising the Lookout."

"Come on in," I said laughing. "Mrs. Chisholm is one floor up. Thanks for coming, Gerry. I'll do you a favour sometime."

"You could do me one right now. I'd kill for a gin and tonic."

"I don't think you'll have to do that," I said as I ushered him upstairs and into the bedroom.

"How do you do, Gino," said Mrs. Chisholm, extending her hand to shake. "So good of you to come all this way."

"My pleasure, Ma'am." He gave a slight bow.

I had to admit Gerry cut quite a dash. Dressed entirely in his customary black, he had tinted his short beard and equally short hair a becoming shade of old gold. Short, compact, dense, he radiated energy. His large hazel eyes inspired trust. Clients opened their hearts to him and spilled secrets they would hardly have admitted to their best friends.

"Gino, would you like a cigarette?" asked Mrs. Chisholm. "I certainly would."

"No thanks, I don't smoke."

"In that case would you like a drink?" she asked.

"A gin and tonic sure would hit the spot."

"Gemma, would you be good enough? I think you'll find everything you need in the bar."

By the time I had brought the drink upstairs, Gerry had combed out Mrs. Chisholm's hair and was studying her from different angles.

"You want to be able to wash, comb, and forget about it. What do you think, Gemma? Shingled—with bangs?"

"Oh dear," Mrs. Chisholm exhaled sharply, "I'm too old to look like Louise Brooks, and I don't want to resemble a Skye terrier."

"You won't. Trust me."

I draped Mrs. Chisholm in a sheet, and Gerry went to work. He certainly knew his way around a haircut, and in short order the white hair lay smooth and snug on the sides and back of the head, softly feathered in front. Just before positioning Mrs. Chisholm so she could see the final result, I quickly made up her face.

"All right," I said, "have a look." I turned on the lights so she could see her reflection in the mirror over the dresser.

The transformation was quite astonishing, not that Mrs. Chisholm seemed younger. She looked her age, but with style. Gone was the appearance of a woman beaten down by years of chopping wood for the stove and washing clothes by hand in the river.

"I feel like Bernice in that Fitzgerald story, 'Bernice Bobs Her Hair.'" she laughed. "Should I be formally introduced to the woman in the mirror? Remarkable, quite remarkable."

Behind her back I winked at Gerry.

"Older women should wear their hair short," he said. "If I had my way I'd put a notice in with every woman's first old-age pension cheque: Have you had your hair cut recently?"

"Will you have another drink?" she asked him.

"Perhaps he has plans for the evening," I volunteered, giving him a chance to escape.

"Not at all," he replied. "I'd love another. The heat's been off in my apartment for two days—the furnace predates Jacques Cartier. Thank God it's not February, but it's still pretty glacial. If it isn't fixed soon we'll have to break the lease, but the landlord is a c— a creep," he emended, catching himself just in time.

"That must be most unpleasant, sleeping in a cold apartment," said Mrs. Chisholm. "Why don't you stay here for the night? There's room upstairs. Do we have some dinner to spare?"

"Plenty," I replied.

"Why, thank you, Ma'am," said Gerry. "May I use the phone? I'll have to call my roommate to tell him I won't be home."

"If your roommate is confined to that cold apartment, perhaps he would like to spend the night here as well. I presume he won't depart with the flat silver."

Gerry laughed, showing his even white teeth. "No, I'll vouch for that. You're sure we won't be in the way?"

"In a house this size with only two women rattling around? I'll feel far more secure with two men under my roof."

"Why doesn't he come up for dinner?" I suggested. "The roast will easily serve four."

"We'll have a party," commanded Mrs. Chisholm, "to celebrate my new look. I shall put on a clean robe and come downstairs."

"I'll get dinner started," I said. "Gerry, why don't you use the phone in the kitchen. You can top up your drink at the same time."

Gerry sat at the kitchen table, sipping his gin and tonic, while I covered the beef tenderloin with strips of bacon.

"This is really great, Gemma. A freezing apartment is no picnic."

"I'm delighted you're staying over. And Mrs. Chisholm is starved for diversion."

"How come you're looking after her? You've never struck me as a—a woman's companion. She isn't incontinent or anything, is she?"

"No, thank goodness."

"You're lucky. 'Waste is a terrible thing to mind.' I read that in a public toilet once."

We both laughed out loud. "I don't have to clean up after her," I continued. "And a job is a job, even if it is only for two weeks. I'm not exactly flush at the moment, and this chance turned up. The problem remains as to what I am going to do after this gig is over."

Gerry shrugged. "Something will turn up. It always does."

"I used to believe that. Which, I suppose, is another way of saying when you are young you make your own luck. But I'm no longer young, Gerry. I'm not old; I still have my own teeth and hair, but for the first time in my life I have to face the fact that time is beginning to run out. I'm going to have to depend more on myself and less on whatever man happens to be in the picture. Men will become more scarce. Those who aren't gay or nursing wounds from a messy divorce are mostly interested in chicks, girls in their late teens, early twenties. A hen, even one who still continues to lay, gets second billing."

Gerry made a face. "You should marry some middle echelon executive on the way up. You'd make the perfect wife. You're ornamental, you can cook, entertain, be a five thousand horsepower hostess. You know how to make a house liveable. You'd be a great asset, if you could keep from dying of boredom."

"You paint a rosy picture. And how I'd love to meet just such a needy case. I never thought seriously about marriage before now; I always figured it would cramp my style. It seemed a high price to pay for security. Now I'm not so sure. If the right man came along I'd marry him in a second. Because, as I have learned too late, nothing cramps your style more than having to get up every morning and go to work."

"You've noticed."

I slid the roast into an oven preheated to 450° F. (I still cook with ounces, tablespoons, Fahrenheit.)

"I know I'm trying to fight City Hall, but I always believed in having plenty of options. I wanted to try everything, and I don't mean that in a nudge-nudge, wink-wink sort of way. I paid my way through nursing school by working as a waitress. Please don't tell more than your twelve best friends, but I never minded being a sex object. I was going with a guy once who ran a little theatre group, and I actually played Hedda Gabler. I got laughs, but I looked great in the costume. I once ran around with an artist. I used to pose for him and his friends, as a life model, in the buff. I didn't mind sitting still for long stretches of time, but it was awfully chilly. Lofts generally are. I sat at a table in the Act Two café of *La bohème*, draped in a ratty boa. I played the triangle in a symphony orchestra—I was dating the conductor—and I actually came in on time. I took riding lessons while I was seeing a rider on the Olympic team; something about those boots really turned me on. I worked in a health food store where we sold hash brownies under the counter, and I marched for freedom of choice wearing a sandwich board that read 'Bomb the Ban.'"

I filled a large saucepan with water. "I've done a lot of things, Gerry, and I've had plenty of good times. But I have the uncomfortable feeling time has run out, and I have to pay the piper, only he won't take a credit card."

Gerry made a wry face, pulling down the corners of his mouth and wrinkling his forehead. "I'd say it sounds like the fable of the ant and the grasshopper. But what only a few people know is that the ant got stepped on, while the grasshopper hitched a ride to Florida for the winter in a shipment of MacIntosh apples. I have faith in you, Gemma. Anyone with hair your colour can move mountains."

"The truth is that I had better move my buns and get the potatoes on. Then I'll go and see if Mrs. Chisholm is ready to come down. When Luc arrives take him upstairs. You'll be sleeping on the third floor."

"Do you suppose I could have another of these?" He held up his glass.

"Go ahead. Who's counting?"

I wished I had thought to order fresh parsley to chop in the food processor and sprinkle over the new potatoes. Perhaps a little paprika would make them look less naked.

Six

I tend to sleep fitfully in a strange bed. In the past my lack of sleep could often be blamed on an enthusiastic partner waking me at all hours. The first night in an unfamiliar house, for which I was responsible, had the same effect. I drifted in and out of sleep, and awoke earlier than usual to the promise of a bright, beautiful day.

I went directly to the kitchen to start the coffee, then up again to Mrs. Chisholm's room. To my surprise she was wide awake, sitting up in a chair, smoking the first cigarette of the day.

"Good morning, my dear. I hope you slept half as well as I." She reached up to pat her short bob. "It felt so odd to wake up without my hair."

"I'll bring you some coffee."

"I can't remember when I've enjoyed myself so much," she went on. "What charming young men. And when did I last drink champagne?" She was still smiling to herself in recollection as I left the room.

Downstairs the mood was definitely more sombre. Luc, Gerry's lover, who also worked at Tresses and Ton-sure, suffered under a king-sized hangover. Gerry had not even appeared.

"Coffee will be ready in a minute," I sang out.

He ran a hand through artfully frosted hair. A blue-black beard line made his pale skin seem even paler. "I feel like something from the wax museum. I made the mistake of looking in the mirror, and it's definitely time to redecorate my face."

"Believe it or not, food helps. I'll make you breakfast in a minute."

I took Mrs. Chisholm her coffee, and she requested a poached egg on an English muffin. By the time I returned to the kitchen Gerry had come downstairs.

"Jesus, Gemma, where did you get that *peignoir*? You look as though you should be wearing a blindfold and holding a scale."

"Tut, tut, Ginola," said Luc. "We mustn't make personal remarks, now must we?"

"That's good coming from you," replied Gerry. "You'd tell the Pope his slip was showing."

I laughed out loud. "It is a bit Grecian, I have to admit, but it's less revealing than my other—sleepwear. Are you a little under the weather?"

"You might say."

"This, too, will pass away. I'll heat you some chicken broth, the miraculous cure for which there is no known disease. And something salty is always a help. Then when you've eaten you can take a couple of aspirins."

"Champagne on top of gin? Not smart."

"Not to mention half a bottle of Grand Marnier," added Luc.

"'When liquor comes in the door, judgement goes out the window.'" I tried to keep a straight face. "That's what my mother used to say."

A small spider, almost transparent from a winter of fasting, tumbled onto the table. Momentarily stunned, it took a moment to get its bearing before scuttling towards safety.

"Ohmygod!" squealed Luc. "A spider!"

I reached out for a Kleenex from a box on the counter, scooped up the creature, and flushed it down the toilet.

"My heroine!" he exclaimed. "I can't stand spiders."

Gerry tipped me a wink. "He used to be afraid of flies—until he opened one."

"Up yours!" Luc raised his middle finger.

"Nautical but nice," sang Gerry. "Or can you remember that far back?"

"At least I haven't been phalanxed by the entire army."

"How's Mrs. Chisholm?" asked Gerry.

"Bubbling. She hasn't had such a good time in years. She thinks you're wonderful fun, in spite of your remark about smoking in bed."

"What was that?" asked Luc, wary.

"You told her that if she smoked in bed and set the mattress on fire the neighbours would think she was having really sensational sex. You must remember she's a conservative old lady."

"I'm not so sure," said Gerry. "She's old, true—and she talks like Queen Victoria, but I'll bet you an art deco ashtray she's a lot less conservative than you imagine. I think she's great."

"If you're both feeling under the weather," I suggested, "why don't you fax in sick and spend the day right here? Bloody Marys in front of the TV? Whatever you like, I'll make for lunch. A long afternoon nap? Cocktails? Dinner? I know Mrs. Chisholm would be delighted if you stayed on."

"Evil woman!" Gerry shook an admonishing finger. "Small wonder Adam bit the apple. But I'm afraid duty calls. I'm heavily booked this week, and if I cancel I'll have a hell of a time rescheduling appointments."

Luc put down his coffee with a clatter. "Oh, darling, it must be hell at the top—even if you do eat better. But, like you, I'm afraid I can't disappoint my public."

"Luc, your problem is that you have a heart of gold, hard and metallic."

"Fuck you," retorted Luc, looking at his watch. "What do you say, Ginola? Shall we share a cab?"

"I suppose."

I set two servings of scrambled eggs onto the table. "Eat this first. By the way, how much do I owe you for the haircut?"

Gerry waved his hand. "The house call is on the house. We got room, board, an open bar—pretty fair trade-off I'd say."

"Let me pay for the cab." I took money from the envelope Mrs. Blake had left. "There's plenty more where this came from. Will you be back for dinner tonight? I hate to think of you cooking a chicken on a coathanger over a sterno stove."

"Depends on whether or not we have heat at home. And we're supposed to go to the ballet tonight. Why don't I call?"

After waving the boys out the door (why is it that adult male homosexuals are always called the boys?) I went up to Mrs. Chisholm's room.

"Mrs. Chisholm, I would like to go out this morning to run some errands, go to the bank and the grocery store. Will you be all right by yourself for a couple of hours?"

"Will you be taking a taxi?" she asked.

"I expect so."

"Could I come along for the ride? It's a beautiful day, and it seems like ages since I left the house. Would you mind awfully?"

"Why would I mind? I'd love to have company. In fact, I have an even better idea. Why don't I order a limousine to pick us up, wait for us while we shop, then drive us back up the hill. You'll be far more comfortable than in a grubby taxi."

"What a good idea. I'll wear my gray wool dress. I think you'll find it in the closet upstairs, if you'd be good enough. And after my shower perhaps you'd help me dress and make up. I have to live up to my hair."

"I'll go and order the car," I said.

After going through the closet in the tower room twice, I still could not locate a gray wool dress. Then it occurred to me that some of Mrs. Chisholm's clothes were probably kept in closets on the third floor, now that the rooms were no longer in regular use.

I went into the bedroom nearest the stairs and opened the closet door. At the sight of the contents I could not stifle a small gasp. It looked as though Mrs. Chisholm had kept every evening gown she ever owned. Women who have the space generally do, long after the state of their figure has made the garments obsolete. Perhaps nostalgia is the reason. Surely the sensuous feel of a particular velvet, the smooth drape of a heavy satin, the discreet rustle of a favourite silk can recall an occasion—elegant, glittering, even romantic—better than words in a diary.

I ran my hand along the tightly packed gowns. Even partially concealed by polyethylene bags the fabrics—chiffon, velvet, silk, crêpe, shantung, satin—gleamed dully from the recess of the dark closet.

I pulled out a gown at random: the bodice of ruched blue chiffon was held up by the narrowest of shoestring straps, the bell shaped quilted ivory satin skirt falling in symmetrical folds.

Although a gown of the Thirties, it retained an elegance that was timeless. The next gown I lifted out was strapless rich purple silk, with a fitted bodice and a full skirt made up of tiny pleats. In the same garment bag hung the matching full length stole. The garment echoed the Fifties, but a woman with a beautiful neck and shoulders could wear it to a ball this very evening.

It was almost with regret that I shut the closet door. I would have liked to take out all the gowns, one by one, to admire the way one admires a handsome armoire or a fine piece of silver. Do not beautiful clothes, in particular those sewn for formal or ceremonial occasions, represent the pinnacle of civilization?

Hanging in the bedroom closet across the hall were Mrs. Chisholm's street clothes, including the belted gray wool. By the time we had both made our toilets, as the French would say, the limousine was waiting at the door.

It felt good to ride in a limousine again, even though I was not in a position to pay for it myself. One of the many fantasies I spin, all of which rest on a solid foundation of megabucks, is owning a limousine, a real gas guzzler, with matching chauffeur. The chauffeur himself would be tall, dark, handsome, and discreetly randy, fully prepared to service the owner along with the vehicle.

Our first stop was the bank. The driver helped Mrs. Chisholm from the car, and I helped her into the bank. I filled out a withdrawal slip, which Mrs. Chisholm signed. I took the precaution of tucking extra withdrawal slips into my handbag, just in case. I also learned that the joint account, which to my relief was still active, carried overdraft protection, any shortage of funds being covered by automatic transfer from a savings account. With six hundred dollars of Mrs. Chisholm's money tucked securely into my handbag, I felt equal to any occasion.

The next stop on our itinerary was the greengrocer where I ordinarily shop for myself. The shop is run by a Chinese family, and the produce looks as though it was taken out of the ground ten minutes ago. I bought parsley, without which I could not even begin to prepare a meal. Its elegant curled and pointed triple leaf, green, springy, fragrant, looks almost heraldic, more suitable decorating a coat of arms than garnishing a platter of sole.

I chose a head of romaine, its handsome sturdy leaves tapering from pale green to near blue. Pungent endive, creamy white at the base, pale yellow-green around the tip, went into my basket, as did leeks and carrots. I bought lemons, surely one of nature's most perfect creations. I have always regretted not being able to wear lemon yellow, not even in summer. It makes me look jaundiced. Into my cart I piled crimson apples, copper onions, ochre potatoes, mushrooms the colour of putty. Next I chose cucumbers, about which many a rude joke has been told. I've heard them all. The truth remains that men endowed like cucumbers exist mostly in crude stories. Nobody tells jokes about zucchini, which come much closer to the naked truth. Finally I bought grapes, looking like clusters of jade, and a large bunch of feathery, aromatic dill.

I paid cash for my order and tucked the bill safely away. No matter how freely I spent Mrs. Chisholm's money, everything was going to be accounted for. To use a street expression, I was going to cover my ass.

Leaving Mrs. Chisholm smoking contentedly in the limousine, I went next to La Petite Maison des Fromages, a cheese shop run by a pair of very grand young men, one from Belgium, the other from La Beauce. You can spot the Belgian because he gargles his 'r's' in the back of his throat. They ought to have been jewellers, not purveyors of cheese. A wedge of St. Paulin or a round of Boursault is presented as though it were a diamond bracelet which had once belonged to Marie-Antoinette. They also charge jeweller's prices, but I had a comforting wad of cash. I splurged, buying seductive Gorgonzola, mildly adventurous Camembert, conservative old Cheddar, and a wedge of Brie I would bake until it turned soft and runny, almost like a fondue. Even those who profess not to like cheese fall under the spell of warm brie. Grated Parmesan, fresh pasta, and crusty bread joined the pile on the counter. All it took was cash.

Our last stop was at the carriage-trade grocery store where Christine Blake had a charge account. I was almost beside myself as I pushed my cart up and down the red carpeted aisles, while Muzak softly played "The Merry Widow Waltz". I reached for whatever caught my fancy: tins of king crab, jars of French capers, imported British soups, crackers, jams. It was the adult version of being turned loose in a toy store. Pensive in front of the butcher's counter, I chose whatever I wanted, heedless of cost: tender pink calves' liver, succulent slices of veal, tiny bronze lamb chops, lean bacon sliced to the desired thickness, a boneless roast of pork. I bought coffee beans and had them ground. (Mrs. Blake used horrid coffee from a tin.)

At the checkout I added a carton of Camels to the order, which I charged. It was sheer heaven. As a final gesture of goodwill I generously tipped the packer who carried my boxes out to the waiting limousine.

By then it was time to return home. I didn't want Mrs. Chisholm to get overtired on her first outing and I asked the driver to take us back up the hill. After he had carried in the boxes I paid and tipped him, with the virtuous feeling of someone who is doing her bit for the economy. I also took the precaution of getting a receipt.

I asked Mrs. Chisholm if she would like to go up to her room to rest, but she was so stimulated by the outing that she sat at the kitchen table while I unpacked and put away the food. Gerry telephoned to say that he was going to live, and that Luc was still breathing. The heat had been turned on in their apartment, and they had tickets for the ballet. Thanks, but they wouldn't be returning tonight.

I hung up and relayed the news to Mrs. Chisholm, who was visibly disappointed that the boys would not be joining us for dinner.

"Mrs. Chisholm, we have a refrigerator full of food, and it is no more trouble to cook for three or four than for two. Haven't you a friend you would like to invite for dinner tonight? Perhaps someone you haven't seen for a while?"

When confronted by a problem, Mrs. Chisholm inhaled deeply. "I can think of several people. Now that I no longer go out by myself I hardly ever see my friends. Christine doesn't make them feel very welcome."

"Mrs. Blake is hundreds of miles away."

"I could call Poppy Pitfield, but she has no way of getting up here. She has just moved into a residence, which leaves her financially strapped, so she really can't afford taxis. And she's far too tottery to take the bus."

"If you would like to see her why don't I order another limousine to pick her up, wait, and drive her home when she's ready to leave?"

"Wouldn't that be awfully extravagant? I mean paying for a car just to sit outside?"

"What good is money if you can't make it work for you? You're not getting any younger; nor would it seem is Mrs. Pitfield. What matters is getting together, talking, enjoying one another's company. To scrimp on a limousine is false economy."

"You know something, Gemma, you're absolutely right. I'll call Poppy right now." Mrs. Chisholm rose abruptly and went to the kitchen telephone. After a conversation which seemed to make more sense to the participants than it did to me, it was decided that the limousine would call for Poppy Pitfield at half-past five.

So excited was Mrs. Chisholm at the prospect of seeing her old friend that she had to be coaxed into taking a nap. But I was firm; euphoria is not energy. And I controlled the cigarettes. The promise of a post-nap cigarette propelled her up the stairs and into bed, where she was asleep in seconds. That gave me a chance to read the paper and give some thought to tonight's menu.

As my friend Gerry might have said, Poppy Pitfield was 'to die,' meaning she dressed with a kind of postmodern eccentricity. Under a coat of black Hudson seal, whose worn spots had been touched up with a felt pen, she wore a black cocktail dress, its low square neckline trimmed in jet beads and sequins. Partly from modesty, but more I suspect to stave off the March chill, she wore a black T-shirt under the dress, which matched the black cardigan she wore draped over her shoulders like a cape. Her obviously dyed black hair was pulled severely back into a bun, stark against a face organized around three brilliant spots of colour, a crimson mouth and two peacock blue eyelids. Rock crystal earrings dangled on either side of a velvet choker embroidered in jet beads.

I helped Mrs. Pitfield off with her boots and on with a pair of antique but still elegant satin pumps, which she had brought in a brown paper bag.

"Why don't you go into the living room, Mrs. Pitfield. I'll bring Mrs. Chisholm downstairs."

"Just hang my coat anywhere, Miss . . . ?"

"Johnstone."

"Miss Brownstone."

I steered her over to the *bergère*. "May I get you something to drink?"

"Not too much now."

"A glass of sherry perhaps?"

"I don't much care for scotch," she replied as she smoothed the folds of her skirt and adjusted her cardigan.

"How about a gin?"

As I said the word "gin" Mrs. Pitfield looked directly at me, more precisely at my lips. "A gin would be lovely," she replied. "I used to drink it whenever I had my period, but I no longer have that excuse." She laughed, a deep baritonal rumble. Lipstick coated her two front teeth.

Without raising my voice I carefully enunciated, "With tonic, bitter lemon, water?"

"Just plain, please."

This brief exchange showed me Mrs. Pitfield was what is now called hearing impaired. I brought her a gin before going upstairs to fetch Mrs. Chisholm, whom I had made up and dressed in a mulberry velvet housecoat, bought, she told me, for occasions such as these. She also told me this was the first time she had worn the robe, mute testimony to her curtailed social life.

"Did I warn you?" she whispered to me on the landing, "that poor Poppy is deaf as a post?"

"I figured that out for myself," I replied, "but she seems adept at reading lips."

The two old ladies fell upon each other with glad cries of welcome and little explosions of pleasure. "How wonderful to see you!" "It's been so long!" "You're looking wonderful!" "I love your hair!" "I can't wait to hear all your news!"

The lines were none the less heartfelt for being interchangeable.

Once the initial flurry of excitement had subsided, I settled Mrs. Chisholm in the Morris chair facing her friend. I brought her a glass of sherry and an ashtray, lit her cigarette, and retired to the kitchen. I had decided to serve the veal in a sauce of white wine and mushrooms, with a little pasta, farfalle perhaps, followed by a salad of romaine and endive in vinaigrette. During the salad course I would bake the piece of brie to spread on thinly sliced French bread. Finally I would put out grapes and a plate of sweet biscuits. That should hold the old dears for the nonce.

Just before cooking the veal I went to check on the ladies. At the door of the living room I paused for a second to survey the scene. Left to themselves, the two women communicated easily. Mrs. Chisholm spoke low, enunciating each word slowly and carefully. Mrs. Pitfield, on the other hand, could not really hear herself speak; her voice rose and fell in volume like that of an announcer on a cheap transistor radio. They appeared to be discussing mutual acquaintances. I gave them each another drink, and lit a second cigarette for the hostess. As they were obviously having a good time I decided to delay dinner. We had no deadline to meet. I poured myself a vodka on the rocks and switched on the kitchen radio to hear the news.

A second refrigerator in the basement had been stocked with wine, and I uncorked a bottle to go with the veal. Not quite plonk, not really vintage, the wines went with the rest of the house, adequate but not really good. It was an attitude I found unfathomable. Imagine being able to afford the best, yet making do with inferior quality. What is even more irritating is turning this stupid self-denial into a virtue, almost as if the road to salvation were paved with cheaper brands and discount coupons. It has been observed that youth is too valuable a commodity to be wasted on the young. By the same token I firmly believe money is generally wasted on the rich. Then again, had I not always spent every cent at hand perhaps I wouldn't be cooking veal scallopini for two old ladies presently getting tight in the parlour.

Dinner was delicious. We ate at the kitchen table rather than in the dining room. The pine table, set with linen placemats and softly candlelit, looked very appealing. Mrs. Chisholm ate sparingly, but Poppy Pitfield tucked into her food with quiet voracity. It was not until I served the brie, warm and succulent from the oven, that conversation resumed.

"Tell me, dear," began Mrs. Chisholm once she had caught her friend's attention, "how do you like life in Maple Grove Manor?"

"I love it." Mrs. Pitfield put down her knife and took a swallow of wine. "I confess I was a bit apprehensive about moving. I have always been a woman who valued her privacy, or so I thought. But I had no idea how bored I had become with myself until I gave up my solitary life and moved in with other people. Books and television are a poor substitute for human contact—not that you can't have both. I can remain in my room if I want solitude, but there is always company on the other side of the door. I have even been able to start playing bridge again." She paused to spread brie on a slice of bread.

"I had grown weary of cooking for myself, but my little shopping trip each morning to buy a chop or half a pound of hamburger was often my sole contact with other people. And when the weather was cold, or icy, I hated going out at all. Why doesn't Miss Brownstone bring you by for a visit so you can see for yourself?"

"It's Johnstone," corrected Mrs. Chisholm, but Mrs. Pitfield had turned her attention to the grapes.

"Shall I get your coat, Mrs. Pitfield?"

"Would you be kind enough to fetch my coat, Miss Brownstone?"

"Here, let me hold it for you."

"If you wouldn't mind holding it for me; I have arthritis in my shoulders."

"Let me help you with your boots."

"I hate to ask, but could you give me a hand with my boots? The trials of old age . . ."

After a few more *nonsequiturs* I delivered Mrs. Pitfield to the limousine driver, who had refused my suggestion to watch TV in the den while we ate. I paid for the car with more of that lovely money that was burning a hole in my handbag, and Mrs. Pitfield was whisked away, waving from the rear window like visiting royalty.

"Are you ready to go to your room, Mrs. Chisholm?"

"I would prefer to sit in the kitchen while you tidy up."

"Would you like some tea, or another glass of wine?"

"Wine, please—half a glass."

I poured us each wine and put cigarettes, matches, and an ashtray within her reach.

"It was good seeing Poppy again," she began, inhaling thoughtfully. "We go back a long way. I was her maid of honour when she married Robin Pitfield. You know something, Gemma? I've had more fun—yes, fun—since you came to the house than I've had in a long time, even since before I had pneumonia. Christine is impatient with my friends. She doesn't make them welcome here, and she always seems to be busy whenever I suggest she take me out. The only time I ever leave the house is to see the doctor or the dentist, or to have my eyes tested; maintenance calls, as though I were a broken-down appliance."

I began to load the dishwasher. "You heard what Mrs. Pitfield said about life in Maple Grove Manor. She was terribly reluctant to move, but now she loves it."

"I don't suppose there would be any harm in paying her a visit, but of course Christine wouldn't hear of my moving out." As was her custom when thoughtful, Mrs. Chisholm inhaled deeply. "She would be far too concerned about what other people would think. 'That great big house? And she puts her mother into a home? Whoever heard of such a thing?' And Christine does have power of attorney."

"A power of attorney can always be revoked," I said casually as I scraped the remains of salad into the garbage.

Mrs. Chisholm looked at me as though I had just suggested tearing up the Constitution or revoking the Declaration of Independence. The enormity of the idea made her speechless.

"It would seem to me, Mrs. Chisholm, that when your daughter returns there will be issues to resolve. Are you prepared to move back upstairs? Will you stop seeing your friends? And what about smoking? Are you going to give it up?"

Mrs. Chisholm did not reply. It was evident the prospect of challenging her daughter distressed her. Some people naturally shy away from confrontation. From the very first interview I had Christine Blake pegged as a bully, one who relished imposing her will on those around her. Even had my childhood not been influenced by the aftermath of the war, I would still dislike any hint of fascism. It would delight me to see Christine Blake put to flight. Moreover, I was growing fond of the old lady. Before I left the job I would like to see her comfortably settled for what remained of her life.

I pressed a switch, and the dishwasher sprang to life with a roar. "I guess anything else can wait until tomorrow morning," I said as I surveyed the room.

"You're such a wonderful cook, my dear, and so handy around a kitchen. I don't wish to be indiscreet, but I find it astonishing you never married."

"I wasn't the marrying kind, I suppose. Some women are cut out for marriage. You can tell by the time they are eight years old that they face a future of diaper pails and chocolate chip cookies. Besides, as I once read somewhere, most husbands are like junk bonds; they have no principal, no interest, and they never mature."

Mrs. Chisholm laughed; smoke shot from her mouth in short puffs. "You make it sound quite dreadful. Then again, I suppose marriage is a dreadful institution. Women of my generation were brought up to want and expect everything, the security of an arranged marriage along with the excitement of an affair. And we all married men who were considerably older. Those who

didn't get divorced ended up widowed. At a time in your life
when you most need companionship you find yourself alone, or
else surrounded by other women. One of the drearier aspects of
growing older is that you never get to meet any men, except for
doctors. I'm not looking for romance, I hasten to add, but I like
men. I like their company. I like the way they think, the way
they talk. Most women my age talk only about their grandchildren, or their medication, or how virtuously they have
restricted their salt and sugar intake. Even poor dear Poppy has
become a bit of a bore." She butted her cigarette thoughtfully.

"Would you like to watch television in the den for a while?"

"No, thank you, dear. It's been a full day for me, unaccus-
tomed as I am to life in the fast lane. I think I'll turn in."

After settling my charge for the night, I moved slowly
through the ground floor turning off lights. Far below the house,
city lights glimmered with invitation. Slipping easily into my
fantasy, I imagined living in this house, high above the city yet
still at its centre, only a taxi ride away from the better stores. To
be able to move from floor to floor, not merely from area to area.
How rewarding it would be to decorate a house this size, to put
one's stamp on the large, pleasant rooms. To live in peace and
grace; the very luxury of the idea filled me with a curious nostalgia,
a regret for something I had experienced only in my imagination.

And yet I could not honestly say that life had sold me short.
I have known more than my share of men and good times, along
with their complement of loneliness and concern about the rent.
At least I had lived my life as it flowed past. But just as I was
about to wind down, to draw a deep breath and hang up my hat
(Do you suppose hats will really come back?), I found myself
playing the role of impoverished widow without even the benefit

of status.

In contrast, Mrs. Chisholm, able to purchase anything she could possibly want, was grateful because she had spent the last two evenings with company, not alone in her room. A shopping trip in a limousine was a major outing, to have her hair cut a milestone. She was turning out to be a pleasure to work for, undemanding, easy to please—with the almost predictable result that I was more anxious to extend myself for her than had she proved exacting.

The two days I had been on the job sped by. I had been neither bored nor taxed. Only twelve more days to go, and then what? The future loomed with uncertainty. Oh well, something was bound to turn up. It did for Mr. Micawber, so why not for Gemma Johnstone. Unwilling to hazard further speculation, I switched on the television set. Something about those flickering images banishes thought, like liquor or valium; and it is far easier on the system.

Seven

By now more used to both the house and the unfamiliar bed, I slept deeply. When I finally made my way down to the kitchen the coffee was already made, and Mrs. Chisholm sat at the table, smoking her first cigarette.

"I suppose you're going to scold me," she began, "for coming downstairs by myself."

"Not at all. You're over twenty-one. However, I would hate for you to fall and put a crimp in the activities we have planned."

"I was very careful. I gripped the bannister and took the stairs one at a time. I wanted my coffee, and I did not want to wake you."

"That's what I'm here for. Would you like eggs for breakfast?"

"Not this morning. What I would like is a grilled cheese sandwich. And if you'd be good enough to fetch the newspaper I'll look at it while I smoke a cigarette."

While Mrs. Chisholm chewed her way through the sandwich, grilled on bread toasted first so as to be deliciously crisp, I asked if she had plans for the day.

"As a matter of fact, I think it's high time I bought some new clothes. If I am to continue going out, I want to look my best. I haven't bought anything in over a year except nightgowns and robes, and even those I didn't choose for myself."

"Mrs. Chisholm, have you ever been a blonde?"

"Oh, my goodness no. My hair was auburn before it turned white. Why?"

"Every woman ought to be a blonde at least once in her life. We could go by the shop and have Gerry give you an ash blond rinse."

Mrs. Chisholm looked alarmed. "What happens if I don't like it?"

I put down my cup. "I have an even better idea. We'll buy you a wig. With your short hair it will be very easy to put on. And why only one? You could be a blonde, or a redhead like me—we'll pass for sisters—or auburn, the way you were. You could choose your hair to go with your clothes."

Mrs. Chisholm inhaled deeply. "My goodness, Gemma, I really don't know. I don't suppose it would hurt to look." She burst out laughing. "When Christine talked about hiring a companion I thought I would be stuck with a dun-coloured widow, or a spinster, who would be punctilious about maintaining the status quo: meals on a tray, games of cards or scrabble, a kind of mousy deference, or—worse still—someone who would tell me at length all about her boring and predictable life."

"I am a spinster, Mrs. Chisholm."

"Only in the legal sense. Anyone as beautiful as you has to have led a very eventful life. You also keep your own counsel. It is women like you, who don't tell tales, who are the ones with tales to tell."

I gave a Cheshire cat smile and changed the subject. "Would you like to invite someone for dinner this evening?"

"I hadn't really thought about it. You have already cooked lovely meals for company two nights in a row. Wouldn't you like a night off?"

"Not at all. I like to cook, and I will be making dinner for the two of us."

"As a matter of fact, I would love to invite my grandson Timothy, that's my son Brian's boy. He's studying at McGill University and shares an apartment with another student. I seldom get to see him. Whenever he comes all the way up here, summoned by his Aunt Christine, he climbs the stairs dutifully to pay me a visit. But he can never stay long as his presence is demanded downstairs. He's a lovely boy, young man I should say; by far my favourite relative."

"Then why not ask him for dinner? If you telephone now you may catch him before he goes to class."

"You're right. If you would give me a hand going upstairs, I have his telephone number in my night table."

I had just seen Mrs. Chisholm through her shower when the cleaning woman rang the bell at the kitchen door. She wore sneakers, a blue bandanna tied around her hair, and an expression of such professional meekness that I knew one day she would inherit the earth. Probably just as well, as on a salary of sixty bucks a day she would never get to buy it.

"Good morning, I am Miss Johnstone," I said by way of breaking the ice. "I have been left in charge while Mrs. Blake is away."

"I'm Thelma," she said without elaboration, as she went straight to the coffee machine and poured herself a cup.

"Mrs. Chisholm and I will be going out this morning. Will you please change her bed and clean her room and bathroom. She is now on the second floor. And two of the beds on the third floor have been slept in. Please make them up fresh. For the rest, I am sure you have your routine. Please do Mrs. Chisholm's room this morning so it will be ready when she comes back."

The woman neither replied nor looked at me as she took out a frying pan into which she cracked three eggs. As the limousine was due shortly I had to get ready, but as I left the kitchen my shit detector gave a couple of beeps.

The limousine waited at the door as Mrs. Chisholm and I, dressed to go out, made our way down the stairs. The driver headed downtown and eased to a stop in front of a dress shop just off Sherbrooke Street. We entered the sacred precincts of Judith Chalmers Dresses as though going into a vestry. Taste and discretion almost smothered the prospective buyer. Deep pile carpet absorbed noise. Indirect lighting minimized crow's feet around eyes and crepe under chins. Votive saleswomen, no longer young and dressed in understated earth tones, offered sensible suggestions in modulated voices. Comfortably seated in an armchair, Mrs. Chisholm had only to shake her head to have the outfit whisked away on its padded hanger and another held up for approval.

By the time Mrs. Chisholm had chosen a suit, three daytime dresses, and a variety of blouses and skirts; stood patiently while the garments were pinned for alterations; and arranged to have the clothes charged on her account, it was time for lunch.

More than anything in the world Mrs. Chisholm wanted a cigarette. We stood in the street while she lit up. "Women of my generation would never smoke in the street," she laughed, "and look at me now. Where shall we go for lunch?"

"Would you like to return home? There is plenty of food."

"Not at all. It's so good to be out. I used to love the dining room at the Ritz. Shall we give it a try?"

The Ritz sounded just fine to me, and we were soon settled comfortably into a banquette in the smoking section, studying menus.

A man approached our table. Once handsome, his face was now a diary of mornings after. "Hello, Gemma, good to see you."

"Ian!" I offered my hand to shake. "It's been a while. Ian Anderson, I'd like you to meet Mrs. Chisholm."

Heads were bobbed, murmurs exchanged.

"You're looking well, Gemma. Is the world treating you okay?"

"Can't complain. And you?"

"Not too badly. I went through a bad patch, but things have straightened themselves out."

"I'm glad to hear it."

"Well, I have to get back to my table. Nice to meet you, Mrs. Chisholm. See you around, Gemma."

"I hope so."

He returned to his table at the far side of the dining room.

Mrs. Chisholm smiled. "A former admirer?"

"What makes you ask that?" I inquired, picking up the menu I had laid aside.

"He was so ill at ease. Men of his sort are only comfortable around a woman before they have been to bed with her. After the fact they are always uneasy. They have been knocked off their pedestal, and they know it."

I laughed in spite of myself. "You seem to know a great deal about the subject."

"More than I was brought up to know, you may be sure." She

inhaled deeply and took another swallow of sherry, that most lethal of wines.

Something about a banquette encourages confidences. What two women seated side by side in a restaurant, sipping wine and about to embark on a leisurely lunch, have not slipped into a confessional candour, admitting things about themselves they would certainly never mention at breakfast and probably not over dinner.

"I suppose I shouldn't tell you this," she began, "but it's an open secret. My late husband was not Christine's father. Desmond Chisholm was a career naval officer, from a good family. He was considered a catch, and I have to admit he looked very dashing in his uniform—what man doesn't. I was young and inexperienced; it was easy for me to convince myself I was in love—with the brass buttons and gold trim and good tailoring, if not with the man himself. During our early years together he was away a good deal. We had a series of honeymoons but no real marriage.

"Then he was posted here at home for a couple of years, and I ran headlong into that career service mentality. Brian was born, and the preoccupation of a first child kept me from going crazy. Then Desmond was posted to the West Coast, and I felt as though I had been let out of prison. I fell in love again. It was only a brief liaison, but Christine was the result. There was no way I could juggle the calendar, and I was terrified of a back alley abortion. So I brazened it out."

Helen paused to light a cigarette. "Desmond was not at all pleased. He carried on like a character in a melodrama. I was a fallen woman, a disgrace to my sex. He had devoted his life to his country, and this was his reward. We divorced, at a time when divorce was still considered slightly scandalous. I tried to protect

Christine, but people have a way of divulging unpleasant truths, for your own good naturally. I don't think she has ever really forgiven me. But even though she may have had to put up with a good deal of grief, frankly, I'm tired of being made to pay."

"If you will excuse my speaking out of turn," I began after the waiter had taken our order, "I wonder if you wouldn't be better off living away from your daughter. Why burden yourself with old animosities? Just getting through the day is enough of a chore without starting off with a handicap."

The arrival of wine, which we had recklessly ordered, saved her from the necessity of a reply.

As we spooned our quiet way through lobster bisque, I thought about Mrs. Chisholm having to face an irate husband with a baby conceived during his absence. It could not have been easy for a woman raised to be respectable the way some are chosen to be dancers, a conditioning which begins in childhood. What does a fallen woman say in her defense when accused in high moralistic fashion by a man who was obviously a fool? The truth in these cases is too damaging to be spoken, even in anger, so she remains silent or takes refuge in the safety of lies. And all because for one brief instant she felt the pull of something so intense she was prepared to gamble and lose. But love is always a gamble, a game played with loaded dice and a marked deck. Even if you play a winning streak, sooner or later it runs out.

When my first love, a philosophy student, told me he was going to become a priest I was too devastated to argue. I knew him well enough to realize he meant it. He might just as well have died. That the first man I had ever slept with would walk away to embrace a life of celibacy in the cloistered austerity of an all-male society left me at a total loss—for words, for attitudes, for defenses.

I was young, open and trusting where love was concerned.

I realize now that had James not entered the priesthood I would have lost him eventually anyway. At the time I found his sexual reticence refreshing. He was one of the few men I had ever met who did not come on to me. It was I who made the first move. I thought him shy. Perhaps I can even laugh about it now. He made his accommodation with something he suspected about himself and could not accept. So he retreated from life into the closet and locked the door.

Not I. In a way he did me a favour, rescuing me from the myth of love. I mean love as the cataclysmic force which is the stuff of fiction, the overwhelming surge of feeling every adolescent girl of my generation yearned to experience. That kind of love brings grief. Moreover, it does not pay the rent.

I was training to be a nurse at the time of the breakup. One of the surgeons, very senior, very married, asked me out. Still numb, I accepted. After a few trysts in motels he suggested I leave home and move into an apartment, for which he would pay the rent. I saw no reason not to comply.

I can still remember how I regretted not being pregnant when James walked away. It was the only time in my life I ever truly wanted a child, as a way of holding on, of keeping him from making this terrible mistake, or at least as a souvenir of our love. Helen Chisholm had a daughter to keep her memory alive; however, the idea of Christine Blake as *memento amore* did not bear thinking about.

Lunch helped down by a couple of glasses of wine had made Mrs. Chisholm almost comatose. I helped her out to the waiting limousine and we were driven back to the house. As we let ourselves in through the front door, the cleaning woman hurried out of the den and into the pantry as though filled with high purpose.

Playing a hunch, I went into the den. On a table beside one of the armchairs facing the television were a remote control, a mug half full of warm coffee, and an ashtray holding a cigarette butted out just after it had been lit. It did not take a genius to figure out the woman had been goofing off, an impression only confirmed by the state of Mrs. Chisholm's bedroom, untouched since we left. I knew without even looking that the rooms on the third floor had not been made up.

Much as I love to spend money, mine or someone else's, I hate to see it wasted. After settling Mrs. Chisholm for her nap, I went down to find the cleaning woman wiping the kitchen counters in a desultory fashion.

"Thelma, I asked you to change Mrs. Chisholm's bed and clean her bathroom while we were out."

The woman steadfastly refused to look at me. "I didn't have time. I have my own work to do."

"Such as sitting in the den, watching TV, smoking, and drinking coffee. You had just lit a cigarette when you heard us come into the house."

Dropping her air of profound meekness, she shot me a look of pure dislike. "I'm entitled to time off for lunch."

"True, but not five hours. Did you change the beds upstairs?"

"I didn't have time."

"Thelma, in a curious way I am grateful to you. Why, you may ask? Because you have given me the opportunity to say something that I've wanted to say since I was twelve years old. Thelma, you're fired!"

"Fired my ass! Mrs. Blake hired me and she's the only one who can fire me."

"That is a mere technicality. I have been left in charge while she is away, and I am the one who is to pay your wages." Opening my purse I counted out sixty dollars which I placed on the counter. "That is for today. You are quite at liberty to return if you wish. However, I have no intention of giving you so much as another dime in wages. And I probably won't even let you into the house. What Mrs. Blake chooses to do when she returns is her business. Now get out!"

"Bitch!" she snarled as she snatched her coat from a kitchen chair where it had been dumped, and headed towards the door, which she wrenched open.

"One word of advice," I called out sweetly, "if you washed your hair once in a while you wouldn't have to wear that dreary bandanna."

The unilateral directive she shouted back echoed in the space between the houses. Aside from the obvious vulgarity, it was an anatomical impossibility. I wanted to point this out, but she was already out of earshot.

After taking clean sheets up to the third floor and changing the beds myself, I took the used linen down to the basement and put a load into the washing machine. Then I looked in on Mrs. Chisholm. She was sleeping heavily, her breathing deep and regular. It was still too early to start preparing dinner and I paused for a moment, irresolute. Should I watch TV or read until it was time to make tea?

It was then the idea struck me. Going quickly up to the third floor, I went straight to the bedroom closet where Mrs. Chisholm's evening gowns hung in their protective bags. Feeling almost like a child turned loose in someone else's playroom, I reached at random for a hanger. Under the plastic hung a gown of white lace with flared cap sleeves and a draped panel on the side. The voluminous skirt had been cut with extra fullness in the back to give the effect of a train. A beautiful dress indeed, but white has never been my colour. Aside from the unfortunate association of purity and innocence, it does not complement my skin.

I returned it to the closet and took down the next hanger. This gown was more to my liking, gold lamé cut low in the back leaving both arms and shoulders bare. The fabric was gathered softly around a vertical band down the front, ending in a gathered peplum flounce around the hips. The straight skirt flared just below the knee and fell into a short train. One could easily imagine Jean Harlow striking one of her elegant, curved attitudes in such a gown.

Even after all this time the lamé had retained its lustre; it shimmered with invitation. Mrs. Chisholm must have been a size fourteen in her prime, although age had shrunk her down to a twelve. I too wore size fourteen. In seconds I had shed my skirt and blouse and stepped into the gold lamé. I had a little trouble fastening the gown in back; no doubt Mrs. Chisholm had a maid to help her dress, but I managed. Like all really well made clothes the gown adjusted itself to my contours. And the generous cut of the skirt more than compensated for my being taller than the real owner.

Above the dresser hung a pine window frame, stripped and waxed, the panes of glass replaced with mirrors. It was an idea whose time had gone, but hanging from the back of the closet door was a long mirror, cheap glass with an unpainted wooden frame. In order to see myself properly I had to turn on the overhead light. Then, dispassionately, I studied my reflection. The gown gave off an unmistakable aura of glamour. On impulse I reached up and unfastened the clip, allowing my hair to fall freely onto my shoulders. My first reaction was that I looked pretty damned good.

Then I took a second, longer look at myself. Under the hard overhead light, in that cheap, unflattering mirror, I still looked good. But the discerning eye could not ignore the unmistakable traces of age: the slight fullness under the chin, a hint of softness around the upper arms, a suggestion of thickening at the waist. Even my creamy skin looked slightly sallow, the almost invisible wrinkles thrown into relief by the unshaded bulb. What could still pass for laugh lines would one day become crow's-feet. I was a woman in her forties wearing a gown from the Thirties. Were I still thirty myself I could have pulled it off. To be sure, lamé is not an easy fabric to wear. Had the gown been of crepe or velvet, in old rose or sage green, I could have lied to myself with more conviction. But drawn by the glitter like a bird to water, I had decked myself out in an uncompromising costume which magnified every defect. The line dividing ripe from gone-by is narrow but real. There was no way of avoiding the unpalatable truth. My assets had peaked.

As if to soften the impact, I switched off the overhead light and turned back to the mirror for one last look. Suddenly I was aware that I was not the only person studying my reflection in the glass.

My first reaction was not of alarm, although perhaps it should have been. Rather, I felt a kind of embarrassment; I was too old to dress up in grown-up's clothing and play at being an adult. I turned to meet the other pair of eyes.

"Hi, I'm Tim Chisholm."

"I'm Gemma Johnstone." I offered a hand to shake which disappeared into his as if it belonged to one of the dolls propped up on the window seat. "I'm taking care of your grandmother while your aunt is away." I laughed a slightly uncomfortable laugh. "I'll bet you're thinking your grandmother takes quite a liberal view of the housekeeper's uniform—but I wanted so badly to try it on."

"Why not. I think you look great!"

His eyes shone with admiration, and from a great height. Tim Chisholm was huge. Well over six feet and broad, he carried his size with a slight awkwardness, almost as if he had walked into a men's store and tried on a body that was several sizes too large. His strong Chisholm features were still modulated by a post-adolescent softness. He wore the uniform of the affluent student: designer shirt over a T-shirt, jeans, carefully soiled top-of-the-line hiking boots. Around his huge wrist I recognized the metal band of a Rolex watch. By the time he had grown into his body and experience had etched his face, he would be a tremendously attractive man.

"I know Gran generally sleeps in the afternoon," he explained, "so I let myself in with the spare key Aunt Christine keeps in the garage. I hope I didn't alarm you."

"Startled perhaps, but not alarmed. You don't look like a cat burglar." We both laughed; his large, deep brown eyes wrinkled at the corners. His teeth were so white they looked like piano keys. "By the way, where is the spare key kept?"

"Under a clay flower pot, just to the left as you go in the door." (Another useful bit of information Christine Blake had neglected to mention.)

"I'd better change and put on the kettle. Your grandmother

likes tea when she wakes up. I have to change back into my civvies."

"Do you have to? I think you look great the way you are."

"Gold lamé is not recommended for kitchen patrol. I might zap myself with the microwave oven. Why don't you plan to join your grandmother for tea. Would you like me to make some sandwiches?"

"If it's not too much trouble."

"No trouble at all. Now, if you will excuse me, I must change."

While the kettle came to a boil I whipped up a plate of ham and cheese sandwiches, leaving the crust on the bread as I knew Mrs. Chisholm would rather smoke than eat. I got her up, combed her hair, freshened her makeup, gave her a cigarette, and invited Tim to come in.

"Gran," he stopped short, "you look different."

"I should certainly hope so. I've had my hair cut, I've painted my face, and I'm smoking a cigarette." She smiled. "Will I have to stand in the corner?"

"No, it's just that . . . I thought Aunt Christine had nixed smoking in the house."

"She has, but she's away."

"You know smoking is very bad for you," he began with the self-righteousness of the young.

"Very bad. But at my age it's not nearly so bad as doing without."

"I'll bring up the tea," I said.

It was just as well that Mrs. Chisholm wanted to smoke and that I wasn't hungry, as Tim seemed to inhale the sandwiches.

"Mrs. Chisholm," I began, "I have a confession to make. I fired the cleaning woman. She is lazy and incompetent, and did not do one of the jobs I asked her to do."

"Good for you," said the old lady. "She always made a sloppy job of doing my room. We used to have a wonderful cleaning woman, a Mohawk, but Christine decided it wasn't politically correct to hire an Indian as menial, so she let her go. It was a shame really. Louise needed the work."

"Have you any idea how I could get hold of her?"

"I may have a telephone number. Would you bring me my address book from the night table?"

I handed Mrs. Chisholm the small, morocco-bound book, its corners reinforced with gold brackets. Tim sat quietly, putting away sandwich after sandwich.

"Here we are. Louise Laplante. Why don't you give her a call and see if she has any free days." Mrs. Chisholm flipped through the pages of her directory. "My goodness, Gemma, in spite of the Grim Reaper having carried off such a number of my friends, there are still so many I would like to see. I don't suppose I'll have time before Christine gets back."

"If I may make a suggestion," I said as I passed Tim the plate of cookies, which he began to munch methodically, "why don't you throw a party and invite all the friends you wouldn't otherwise see? I would suggest a lunch party, perhaps a buffet. Since many older people are apprehensive about going out at night, lunch would suit them better."

Mrs. Chisholm inhaled right down to her navel. "Goodness me, Gemma, it's so long since I had a party I don't know if I'm up to it. It's so much work."

"We'll have it catered. I have a friend who will do a first rate job, if she's free. I'll give her a hand. And I could probably ring in Gerry and Luc to help out. If someone asked Gerry to a party in New Zealand he'd go."

"If you need a bartender, I'd be glad to volunteer," said Tim between bites. "I've tended bar for Aunt Christine's parties."

"Terrific!" I clapped my hands together. "How about this Sunday? For those who don't go to church Sunday can be a very dull day. And those who do will already be dressed up for the occasion."

"Well, I don't know . . ."

"Do it, Gran!" exclaimed Tim, even though his mouth was full. He gave a huge swallow. "Miss Johnstone is right."

I stood. "First, let me telephone my friend who caters and see if she is free Sunday. Then we can give her numbers once you have drawn up a guest list. Do I have your permission, Mrs. Chisholm?"

Tim and I waited while smoke went deep into her lungs. "As they say on television, Gemma, 'Go for it!'"

Tim and I applauded. "I'll go telephone," I said.

"Fran? It's Gemma."

"Gemma, you old roundheel. What's up—or who, as the case may be?"

"Not bloody likely. I've hit the skids, Fran. I'm working as companion-slash-housekeeper for an old lady."

"How the mighty have fallen. And you who were landed gentry, even if most of the time you landed on your back."

"It's only for two weeks. And the old lady has turned out to be a real dear. Her daughter, currently off on a cruise, has been keeping her a virtual prisoner, and I'm doing my best to show her a good time."

"Gemma, honey, your kind of good time would probably finish her off."

"Be quiet and listen. I know this is short notice, but she would like to have some of her friends in for lunch on Sunday. I don't yet know how many; let's say twenty for starters. One, are you booked? Two, can you handle that many?"

"Can I ever! When times are tough one of the first things to go is entertaining for any reason other than business. I'd welcome the job."

"Good. I'll get Mrs. Chisholm to draw up her guest list. As soon as I have definite numbers I'll get back to you. It shouldn't be difficult to cater. The guests will be mostly elderly, many on diets. Food will be secondary for most of them. Lay on whatever help you need. I'll be here. And we have a bartender."

I gave Fran the house telephone number and promised to be in touch. I then phoned Louise Laplante, the cleaning woman. She sounded pleasant and pragmatic, so matter-of-fact I was almost disappointed. (Had I really expected to hear drumbeats in the background, or to see tiny puffs of smoke coming out of the receiver?) Louise said she was working just one day a week and could use extra money. I warned her the job might only be temporary, but that she could come for as many days as were necessary to clean the house thoroughly.

Once the telephone was free it remained only for Mrs. Chisholm to settle down with her book and start inviting people.

Mrs. Chisholm positively vibrated at the prospect of asking her friends to the house. And I could not suppress a little *frisson* of pleasure when I thought how much Christine Blake would have disapproved of her mother's carousing during her absence.

But now I had to think about dinner, and how to fill that

human backhoe that called himself Timothy Chisholm. Staring at the three tiny filets, more than enough for Mrs. Chisholm and myself, I realized that serving Tim a small piece of steak would be like trying to dam the St. Lawrence River with a bag of kitty litter.

As I studied the tins in the pantry I had the brilliant idea of making up a batch of tuna melt to serve as an appetizer. Piled on four slices of toast, the tuna, egg, celery, green pepper, mayonnaise, all topped with grated cheddar, would help to slow Tim down before his tiny filet. Whereas I would have cooked perhaps half a cup of pasta for Mrs. Chisholm and myself, I would empty the entire bag into a large pot.

Tim wandered into the kitchen and put the copy of *Tom Jones* he had been reading onto the table. "Will I be in the way?" he asked.

"Not in the least."

"Gran is busy on the phone inviting friends to her party. She's totally turned on by the whole thing."

"I hope so. What is the point of a party if not to have a good time?"

"She's so different from the last time I came to visit. She seems younger, more interested in things."

I began chopping ingredients into a bowl for the tuna melt. "I think your grandmother was suffering from what psychologists would call sensory deprivation. She was isolated, never going out, not seeing anyone. That is no way to live. Would you like a beer? There's some in the fridge."

Tim lumbered across to the refrigerator and extracted a beer. He talked while I worked. I knew his parents were divorced, but I learned his mother had remarried and moved to Vancouver. He was in his final year of a degree in English and history. Next year he was to begin law school.

I asked if he had studied with Arthur Morris, his uncle by marriage.

"No, I haven't. He teaches twentieth-century drama, which doesn't interest me very much, and he doesn't have much of a reputation on campus. Which is another way of saying he does have a reputation, but not for teaching. He's far more interested in graduate students than in research. I haven't told anyone we're related."

Tim went on to tell me about his cousins, Christine Blake's children: two daughters, both married, both living on the West Coast, and a son, currently studying at Berkeley. He didn't exactly say the children wanted to be as far from their mother as it was possible to get without crossing water, but the subtext was clear.

He talked about his own parents, to whom he was obviously close. Major holidays he spent with his mother on the West Coast. His father, making pots of money in spite of the poor economic climate, frequently came to Montreal on business. It was a while since I had spoken with a young person who could begin entire sentences without using "like" to get the words turning over. I found myself enjoying his company.

I escorted Mrs. Chisholm downstairs to join Tim and set her up with a sherry and a cigarette. It was the kind of meal that required last minute attention, and I find it difficult to cook and chat.

"Gran, I was wondering if I could spend the weekend here. My roommate's girlfriend is visiting from Ottawa, and I'll be very much in the way. I thought with Aunt Christine out of town . . ."

"I don't mind if it's all right with Gemma. She's the one who will be preparing the meals."

"Of course he can stay," I called from the stove. "We might want to rearrange furniture for the party, and he can give us a hand."

"I can drive," he volunteered, "so if there are any last minute errands to run I can zoom down the hill."

"Do you suppose we should telephone the society reporter from the newspaper?" asked Mrs. Chisholm with a laugh. "It will be the social event of the season. By the way, I have twelve definite acceptances, but I still have more calls to make."

"That's fifteen counting you, me, and Tim. Two more if Gerry and Luc decide to come. How many more friends do you have to call?"

"Seven or eight."

"I'll give Fran thirty as a working number. That will give us some leeway, and if there is leftover food we'll send it home with Tim."

"You make it sound so easy," said Mrs. Chisholm after exhaling a long stream of smoke.

"It is, Mrs. Chisholm. All it takes is a few phone calls and some money."

"I suppose. But whenever Christine entertains she insists on doing it all and works herself up into an awful state."

During the pause that followed I served the tuna melt, half a slice each for Mrs. Chisholm and myself, two full slices for Tim. I had warned Mrs. Chisholm of my strategy to fill up her grandson; she ignored her serving and smoked. I ate about half of mine, while Tim, who had been well drilled in good table manners, ate his entire serving. He never wasted time on speech while he ate, thus enabling him to dispatch his food with concentrated efficiency.

"You have no idea what a treat it is to eat food that is hot," said the old lady. "By the time my tray is carried up all those stairs everything is cold, even soup."

"That part of your life is now finished. Here, let me cut that filet for you. These steak knives need sharpening."

"That part of my life is indeed finished. I hope you don't mind taking me out again tomorrow morning. I have a couple of calls I'd like to make."

"Shall I order the car as usual?"

"I don't see why not."

Leaving Tim and Mrs. Chisholm to chomp their way through the salad, I went into the den and ordered a limousine for the following morning. Then I telephoned Fran and told her to plan for thirty people.

"And, Fran, please don't prepare anything that needs cutting. I anticipate an invasion of arthritic hands; it will be all they can do to grasp the plate and wield the fork."

"Not to worry, Gemma. What I have in mind is sophisticated baby food, with steak and kidney pie and steak tartare for those who want something more substantial. Nothing too messy, nothing too unwieldy. Trust *moi*. You're talking to an old pro, honey."

"I know. But at the moment we're talking about cooking."

Fran laughed, a vibrant, hearty sound. "You know what they say: it takes one to know one. Do you want me to call tomorrow and give you a menu?"

"No, thanks. You know your business."

"That's a switch. The last client I worked for wanted to know everything, how many olives in the vegetable tray, whether I used real butter. 'No, Lady, I use the fake.' And whether I made my own mayonnaise. I do, but it costs."

"For Sunday you have no restrictions, so don't cut corners. Pull out the stops, lobster, crab, hearts of palm—the works."

"Sounds good. And if you can pay me in cash I won't have to charge you sales tax. Could I swing by tomorrow maybe and look at the kitchen?"

"Sure thing, in the afternoon. I'll be out during the morning."

My last call was to invite Gerry and Luc. Gerry was delighted at the idea of something to help make Sunday pass.

"Would you feel demeaned," I said, "if I asked you to help out?"

"Hell, no. I much prefer to be a moving target. That way I won't be nailed by a bore."

"Good. Sunday around noon. Come earlier if you can get yourself out of bed."

I went into the kitchen to find Tim on the point of leaving. He had already told me solemnly that he never ate dessert, or anything sweet, citing good nutrition as the reason. I thought of the plate of cookies that had vanished over tea and said nothing. He kissed his grandmother goodnight and said he would see us sometime tomorrow. His monolithic figure moved with steady determination down the crescent, and I returned to the kitchen to see if Mrs. Chisholm was ready to go upstairs.

She chose to have another cigarette. "Sit down, dear," she began, "I have a couple of things I'd like to discuss. Tomorrow I'm going to see my notary to revoke the power of attorney. It's time I took charge of my own life again. Who knows? Maybe Christine and I will get along better when she is no longer in command. Either that or she will be even more difficult to live with than she is now."

"Will you manage your own affairs, or do you plan to appoint someone in your daughter's place?"

"For the moment I will try to operate on my own, with the help of my notary and my investment counsellor. Should I need an attorney I'll ask Tim. He's a responsible young man, and he intends to study law."

"I hadn't thought of Tim," I admitted, impressed by Mrs. Chisholm's sudden burst of enterprise.

"You see, Gemma, I've been doing a lot of thinking." She paused to inhale. "Nothing concentrates thought like a cigarette. I've been living like Sleeping Beauty in the fairy tale, comatose, waiting for someone to come along and wake me up. I was a recluse in my own house, unhappy with the *status quo* and too paralyzed to do anything about it. Then you turned up."

She reached across the table and patted my hand. "You're one of the best things that could happen to me. But you're not going to spend the rest of your life keeping an old lady company. Whatever your reason for taking this job, money I expect, you won't stay. By the way, what kind of salary is Christine paying you, if you don't mind my asking?"

"I'm not certain," I replied with a deprecating laugh. "Mrs. Blake and I never really discussed the subject before she left."

Mrs. Chisholm struck the table with impatience. "Isn't she the limit! So you've been working for nothing, as it were."

"I'm sure we will arrange something when she returns."

"Tell me the truth. You are a registered nurse, are you not?"

"Yes, I am."

"What does an R.N. earn per eight hour shift?"

"That depends on the agency; say, about $150."

"$150? Let's see. You work at least two full shifts a day. That comes to $300, times seven equals $2100. Does $2100 a week seem satisfactory?"

"More than."

"Good. Tomorrow I'll sign another withdrawal slip. You pay

yourself a week's salary, and take whatever money you need for the party. And now I think I'll turn in."

"Would you like to watch television before you go up, Mrs. Chisholm?"

"Gemma, please call me Helen. At this point Mrs. Chisholm seems terribly formal."

"Are you quite certain you want me to?"

"Yes, unless it makes you uncomfortable."

"Not in the least." I smiled. "And you're the boss lady. You call the shots."

"Oh, I hope not. You make me sound like the prison matron in one of those dreadful movies about women behind bars. Gemma, I think I'd like to go upstairs."

"Of course."

"Of course—who?"

"Of course, Helen."

"See? It didn't hurt a bit."

The old lady was on such a roll I couldn't help wondering what would happen when Mrs. Blake got back from her cruise. I confess I rather relished the prospect. Now that I would no longer have to present myself, cap in hand, to Mrs. Blake to request my salary after my services had been rendered, I felt equal to anything. It was as though I were playing a board game, *Monopoly* perhaps, in which I was both a player and a token. I had already passed Go and collected my $200, but whether I would win second prize in a beauty contest or take a walk on the Boardwalk remained to be seen.

Eight

riday morning I abandoned my uniform of skirt and blouse for a rather becoming green silk dress. One never knows when opportunity might knock in the guise of a potential admirer, and I was taking Mrs. Chisholm, or Helen as she had asked me to call her, to confer with her notary. I have never kept company with a notary, although I have known a number of lawyers, one of whom managed to write me off as a tax deduction. I have even made the acquaintance of a couple of judges, who turned out to be quite a handful once they shed their professional gravity. One of them believed that the best things in life are three; and I was obliged on occasion to ring in a 'friend,' one of those pretentious whores who calls herself an actress and model. The second Mr. Justice had a whole string of pet names for his appendage; he must have read *Lady Chatterley's Lover* at an impressionable age. Again it was almost like going to bed with two people as he chatted on about Dick Dork, or Walter Wang, or Peter Prick, all of whom wanted to enter my O-zone. It was very tiresome, but he did give nice presents. And who am I to question the name of a gift horse?

At nine o'clock the kitchen doorbell rang, and I opened it to find a woman in a duffel coat on the doorstep.

"I'm Louise Laplante. You asked me to come today?"

"Yes, I did. Come in, Louise. I'm Gemma Johnstone. As I explained on the phone, I'm taking care of things for a few days. There's coffee. Hang up your coat and have some."

Briefly I filled her in on the situation and asked her to clean Mrs. Chisholm's room and bath while we were out.

"Has the tower room been cleaned up since she moved?" inquired Louise.

"Not really."

"I'll do that next. And if you're having company I'd better clean the ground floor."

"Don't worry about the kitchen," I suggested. "I clean as I go, and it will see a lot of use this weekend. If you wash it down today you will only have to do it again next week. Why make work?"

Louise smiled, showing teeth badly in need of attention. It was a shame, as she was an otherwise attractive woman. Louise was probably the first Mohawk I had ever met, and she was quite unremarkable, except for beautiful cheekbones, the kind that carry a face comfortably into old age. Screen careers have been built on less.

By the time the limousine drew up had Mrs. Chisholm dressed, made up, and ready to go. We drove down Victoria Avenue as far as the abandoned railway station and turned east along St. Catherine Street.

"This stretch looks much as I remembered it," said Mrs. Chisholm, "but Westmount has always resisted change."

"Things get a bit more dreary once we cross Atwater."

"So I've been told." She leaned forward to look out the window as we drove into the urban decay of the strip between Atwater and Guy. "Oh, dear me, it does look derelict. How many times I went to films at the Seville Theatre, and now it looks as if it's about to fall down. This used to be such a vital part of the city. It's sad to see it looking so old and worn. But I suppose buildings age just as people do."

Mrs. Chisholm settled back into the seat until the car pulled to a stop in front of a gleaming office tower. Even though I had made myself up with extra care, I still double checked my appearance in the mirror I always carried in my bag.

My anticipation was short-lived. B.F. Bradley turned out to be crisp, efficient, well tailored, and female.

Mrs. Chisholm explained her reason for the visit. She had come to revoke the power of attorney she had given to her daughter, Christine Blake. She wanted the revocation to be drawn up in a notarized document, with no possibility for loopholes. Ms. Bradley, no doubt accustomed to family fallings-out, inquired merely whether there was anyone she wished to name in her daughter's place.

"Not at the moment," replied my employer.

Ms. Bradley explained she would need time to draft the document, and we agreed to return Monday morning so Mrs. Chisholm could sign it. Once outside the building she lit a cigarette with obvious relief. "And now I'd like to buy some flowers or a plant to take along to Poppy Pitfield. I want to invite her to the party, and I'd like to see the place where she is living."

We drove to Maple Grove Manor, with stops to pick up a white azalea and two cartons of cigarettes. The car turned into the crescent shaped driveway flanked with shrubs and pulled to a stop in front of the main door. Stairs and a ramp led to glass doors which swung open automatically, and the two of us entered the handsomely appointed lobby. Two wing chairs upholstered in chintz faced a camel backed sofa across a low Queen Anne table on which sat a pink cyclamen in full bloom.

To the left was a reception desk where I asked the tailored and smiling receptionist to ring Mrs. Pitfield's room.

Mrs. Pitfield had gone out. Were we expected?

No, we weren't. I returned to Mrs. Chisholm. "Would you care to visit a friend of mine, Valerie Potter? She's the mother of my good friend, Edith Cross, the one who put me in touch with your daughter."

Permission was granted, and we made our way from the elevator along taupe broadloom to Room 219.

Mrs. Potter, a handsome, opinionated woman, has been a sort of surrogate mother to me ever since my own mother died. As I can never be bothered to contradict her, we get along beautifully. With her own daughter Edith, however, meetings turn into one long confrontation—over politics, ecology, Native rights, the Canada Council, or whatever has caught the fleeting attention of the media. Neither woman will admit the antagonism springs from the stereotypical situation of a forceful mother confronted by an equally strong willed daughter, each convinced the other is to blame for whatever disagreements may erupt. Rather than live with Edith in a state of uneasy truce, Mrs. Potter chose to move into Maple Grove Manor, a decision she has never once regretted.

I made introductions and unwrapped the plant. Both old ladies lit cigarettes and became instant allies. Old age brings with it a kind of freemasonry, and in no time the two women were talking as if they had been friends for years. I let them chatter on. Mrs. Potter's appraisal of the residence echoed that given by Poppy Pitfield at our recent dinner.

"We lived in a big house," explained Mrs. Potter. "I kept it on even after the children moved out and my husband died. I don't know why I was so inflexible, but the idea that I would give up my house was quite inconceivable. It was the kind of reasoning that got the British kicked out of India. Fortunately I came to my senses in time. The house had become a burden, and I really didn't want to live with my daughter; she persuaded me to move into Maple Grove. Now I regret only the loneliness of those last years in that big, empty house."

The two old ladies butted out their third cigarettes and I rose, signalling that we were to leave. Mrs. Chisholm invited Mrs. Potter to the party on Sunday. I suggested we invite Edith so she could bring both her mother and Mrs. Pitfield up to the house and see them safely home. Partings were effusive and by the time we peeled ourselves away it was time for lunch.

As we drove up the hill, moving steadily away from shops, restaurants, libraries, Mrs. Chisholm turned to me. "Are there any special requirements for moving into Maple Grove?"

"Only financial. And you have to be well enough to go in under your own steam. Once you are a resident you will be cared for in case of ill health."

There followed a thoughtful silence before the next question. "You can furnish it any way you like?"

"If you wish," I replied. "The rooms are already furnished, but you can bring whatever you want. Did you notice that Mrs. Potter has her own small refrigerator? That means she can keep cheese and fruit. She doesn't have to go down for a meal if she doesn't feel like it."

"How long has Mrs. Potter lived there?"

"Almost three years now. She and her daughter have agreed

to disagree, so she is really far better off in the residence."

The rest of the drive passed in silence. I could tell Mrs. Chisholm's energy was on the wane, and she smoked one last preoccupied cigarette while we returned to the house.

I took Mrs. Chisholm right up to her room. In order to help her into bed I had to turn back covers pulled so taut and tucked in so tightly they would have resonated if struck. The room positively glowed; the bathroom fixtures shone. Furthermore, Louise had brought all Mrs. Chisholm's photographs down from the tower room and polished the frames.

"I wonder if I really want to be surrounded by all those reminders of the past," said Mrs. Chisholm as she pulled on a nightgown.

"If not, I'll put them away for you. But let's wait until Louise has gone home."

Curiosity drove me upstairs to find Louise scouring the tower room.

"I'm just about to make lunch," I said. "Have you eaten?"

"Not yet."

"Give me fifteen minutes to feed Mrs. Chisholm and come on down."

Lunch is the meal that has always tested my ingenuity. Breakfast usually operates within a limited range, even when cooked, while dinner has no limits whatsoever. But lunch remains a problem. We want to eat, but not too much. We want it to be appetizing, but with a minimum expenditure of time. And now that most quick and appealing convenience foods have been stamped as potential killers, the choice narrows even more.

Anything with eggs echoes breakfast; menus with meat, or even chicken, preview dinner. I was turning a couple of tins of crab-meat into a salad when the phone rang. Fran, who was in the neighbourhood, asked if she could drop by and check out the kitchen. I replied that if she came by now I would give her lunch. She gave a whoop and told me I was on.

I had just finished setting Mrs. Chisholm's tray when Louise came into the kitchen. "Let me take that up for you," she suggested. "It will give me a chance to say hello to Mrs. Chisholm."

As I was about to throw some rolls into the microwave, I saw Fran's car pull into the driveway. She teetered up to the door in a pair of high heeled boots which would have done credit to Ilse, She-Wolf of the S.S. I opened the door, and Fran exploded into the kitchen.

"Pardon me, Madame, but didn't you used to be Gemma Johnstone?"

"The very same."

"The Gemma Johnstone I used to know wouldn't be caught dead wearing a butcher's apron over a silk frock."

"The Gemma Johnstone you used to know has gone to her just reward. I'm a born-again cretin. This way to the servant's quarters."

Fran Sullivan is the last of the big-time broads. Hers is a bottom that draws men's hands the way a magnet draws iron filings. Hers is a bosom that inspires the poetry of euphemism: boobs, jugs, knockers, and the rest of those succinct synonyms used by men for whom a bust involves the police. Her eyes, orbs rather, magnified by contact lenses, shaded and outlined like those on an Egyptian frieze, look at the world from beneath an awning of artificial lashes. In repose her face is not beautiful; one might even call her homely. But she has vitality, a volcanic energy that overcomes all obstacles and leaves you with an impression of radiance.

Her third husband, the one she was really crazy about, died of cancer. His death left her low, emotionally and financially, but she rallied and turned a flair for cooking into a small but success-ful catering service. She is the one enduring friend I made at high school.

She was just examining the cupboard holding serving dishes, when Louise came into the kitchen. Both women did what in vaudeville used to be called a double take.

"Princess Laughing Water!"

"White-woman-who-speak-with-forked-tongue!"

They embraced.

"Long time no see," said Fran.

"For many moons," said Louise.

I watched, amused. "I take it you ladies know one another?"

"Do we ever!" replied Fran. "and am I ever glad to see her. Louise, are you working this Sunday?"

"No, why?"

"My niece, who generally works with me, has the flu. We can't have anyone breathing germs over the antique guests, for whom a pulmonary infection could prove fatal. Could you help me out? I will give you beads and trinkets."

"Sure, if it's all right with Miss Johnstone."

"Louise, please call me Gemma. And I think it's a great idea. If you'll stay on and help clean up after the party I'll pay you a day's wages."

"I may not be able to finish cleaning the ground floor today. Could I come tomorrow and work? There will be plenty to do.

You may want silver cleaned."

"By all means come for the day. And now why don't we eat before carrying on with our various tasks. Louise, you know where everything is kept. Would you mind setting the table?"

As my curiosity had been piqued by the way Fran and Louise had greeted one another, I brought up the subject once we were seated around the table.

"Can you believe," Fran laughed her easy laugh, "Louise used to work for me. She was my cleaning lady, and every other inch a lady you may be sure."

Louise smiled. "Everyone who goes out to clean ought to work for someone like Fran. Having worked herself she understands what it means to do a job. She paid me regularly and she was always polite. In no time we had become friends."

"My second husband," began Fran, "was what used to be known as a diamond in the rough. He had *mucho dinero*, but very little else. It was his idea that I engage a cleaning woman, not to save my back and prevent my pretty hands from growing chapped, but because he didn't want it known his wife did her own housework."

Fran paused to refill her teacup. "He was a contrary bastard. The second he learned that someone was Scottish or Jewish or Polish he had to tell an ethnic joke, just to prove that he didn't hold with prejudice. What a laugh. The jokes bubbled with hostility. 'No tickee, no laundry' became his tag line. When he had ring-around-the-collar it was red. He was the one who first called Louise Princess Laughing Water and me the White-woman-who-speak-with-forked-tongue. Those were his milder digs. I remember the day he overheard Louise singing to herself as she worked in the kitchen. He started out by saying she was very hep.

That soon degenerated into heap hep. Louise became the heap hep help. Maybe it was mildly amusing the first time around—all those h's..."

"Alliteration," I suggested.

"That's it!" Fran laughed. "I remember alliteration from high school, one of those bits of information you never, ever use after you graduate. You know something? In all my years of dating I have never once had the chance to say to a guy that 'The square of the hypotenuse on a right-angled triangle is equal to the sum of the squares of the other two sides.'"

"You always did have questionable taste in men," I said, laughing.

"True. Too true. Too terribly true. Is that alliteration, or what? Anyhow, this man—the one I had the bad judgement to marry—got the bit between his teeth about Louise. He never called her by name, always Princess Laughing Water, or Miss Mohawk, or whatever. I remember telling him that his Indian shtick wasn't funny the first time around and, like meat loaf, it didn't improve with age. He was one of those men who wanted desperately to be liked. The slightest hint of criticism meant rejection, and when he felt rejected he turned mean. We had a big row, and he threatened to cut my allowance so I wouldn't be able to pay for a cleaning lady. He always referred to a cleaning 'lady,' not a cleaning woman. That's one of the things the lower classes do when they try to be middle."

We all laughed on cue, but did not speak, as we knew there was more to come.

"I said he was the one who had insisted on my having a cleaning lady and that I was quite capable of doing my own housework. I would also be happy to tell my friends I did my own chores and flaunt my chapped hands and broken nails to prove it. It was just about then that I came to realize he had a problem with the sauce. It was only going to be a matter of time before he got drunk and beat me up, so I split. The best decision I ever made, except that I could no longer afford to pay Louise. She had to find another job." Fran leaned across the table and squeezed Louise's hand. "Isn't that a hoot! I no longer even speak to my ex, but the cleaning lady and her employer have become friends. Moreover, she's going to work for me again. And Gemma, honey, we owe it all to you."

After lunch Louise returned to her Bon Ami and Pledge while Fran and I ventured into the dining room to investigate dishes and flatware. Between the breakfront and the sideboard we found enough china and silver to feed twice the number invited. Mrs. Chisholm must have started married life with a dozen of everything, from lunch plates to soup shells; and when Christine Blake moved in with her mother she brought her own trousseau. A few silly millimetres separate a lunch plate from its dinner equivalent; but there they were, forty-eight plates in all, Aynsley faced off against Royal Doulton.

"'God bless the child that's got his own,'" sang Fran in a cracked contralto.

"It's hell being underprivileged," I echoed. "When Mrs. Chisholm wakes up I'll ask her about tablecloths. There must be a dozen squirrelled away somewhere."

Louise came into the room. "If you want to use linen napkins instead of paper, I can wash and iron them next week."

Fran laughed. "This is going to be a breeze. All I have to bring is the food."

"Do you want some money on account?"

"It would be a help, for those places where I can't charge."

I opened my bag and peeled some bills from the reassuring roll. Many people dislike handling money, especially older bills with their association of greasy hands and germs. My own mother was terrified of germs, convinced that every time I opened the front door thousands of germs, in neat Roman rows, marched into the house and onto the butter, her toothbrush, my pillows. It goes without saying she hated to handle money; if I found a coin in the street it had to be taken home and scrubbed along with the hands holding it. (And when I think of some of the men she slept with . . .)

None of her aversion to money was passed on to me. I love the look of it, the feel, the texture, the colour. (American bills may be worth more, but ours are more beautiful.) I cannot deny the erotic charge that bills of large denomination send through my body. On more than one occasion, when my admirer of the moment looked better in his clothes than out of them, I had only to think of the money tucked discreetly into the Lalique vase and I was able to respond to his embrace with an ardour that was more than merely theatrical. Perhaps that is the reason I have never been tempted by drugs. I get far more of a high from the cash in hand than from any chemicals the money might buy.

The last cleaning woman got sixty dollars for doing nothing. Louise asked for fifty-five; I gave her seventy. Ten dollars an hour for someone who worked as hard as she did was a steal.

I plugged in the kettle and went up to check on Mrs. Chisholm, who was just drifting into consciousness. I was on my way downstairs when the doorbell rang. Thinking it was probably Tim arriving to spend the weekend, I opened the door, a greeting already forming itself.

To my surprise an older man stood on the stoop. "Good afternoon," he said, "I am Brian Chisholm. I've come to visit my mother."

"Good afternoon," I answered, standing aside to let him pass. "I'm Gemma Johnstone. I'm looking after your mother while Mrs. Blake is away." As he came through the door he offered his large hand to shake, the grip cool and firm. "Your mother is just waking up from her nap. Give me a minute to help her get ready, then you can join her for tea." I smiled my most disarming smile and headed up the stairs. Conscious of his eyes following me, I stood tall as I moved carefully up to the landing, one hand resting lightly on the bannister, the other curved over my abdomen.

"You have a visitor," I said as I took Mrs. Chisholm's burgundy velvet robe from the closet. "Your son is here to see you."

"Brian! Here?" Surprise jolted her awake.

"He will join you for tea, the new you that is. Now up you get and into your good robe. I'll comb out your hair and freshen your makeup."

By the time I went down to make tea, Brian Chisholm had wandered into the kitchen to drink a glass of water.

"What brings you to Montreal, Mr. Chisholm?"

"Business, and the chance to visit Mother. Also my son Tim, who is here at university."

"I've met Tim," I said as I scalded the pot. "He came for dinner last night. In fact he's coming up to the house to spend the weekend. I thought it was Tim when you rang the bell. Would you like to stay for dinner tonight? I had planned to cook for Tim and your mother, so you'd be killing the proverbial two birds with one chop."

He smiled. "That sounds delightful. Are you sure I won't be putting you out?"

"Not in the least." I finished setting the tea tray.

"Here, let me carry that for you. It looks heavy."

"Thank you, kind sir." I held open the swinging door and led the way upstairs, silently thanking the Lares and Penates that I was wearing my green silk and heels rather than my decidedly dowdy blouse, skirt, and loafers.

"Surprise!" I announced as we came through the door.

What followed were the usual effusions of mother greeting son whom she had not seen for a while: predictable questions, rehearsed responses to be read and deciphered in the total context. Evident was a real affection, to be gleaned from the silences as much as from the sounds.

My first impression told me that Brian Chisholm was not a demonstrative man. Were I to attempt a portrait, to limn his features as once was said, I would use pastels rather than oils, and from the cool end of the spectrum. He was not without colour, but the tints were muted, pale gray hair, pale beige skin, the palest of blue eyes. The family resemblance resonated. Were one to meet Brian Chisholm at the North Pole and his sister at the South, one would know instantly they were related.

He dressed by numbers, his expensively neutral clothes drawing attention to themselves by their very absence of *éclat*. Like his mother he spoke softly, but I have no doubt that in the boardroom he carried a big stick.

During the pause in the conversation while tea was poured, I told Mrs. Chisholm that her son was staying on for dinner. She expressed delight at the prospect and asked where he was planning to sleep. He replied he had a reservation at his usual hotel.

"Would you like to spend the weekend here, Mr. Chisholm?" I asked. "You could use the tower room, now that it is vacant. You won't be disturbed up there, and we expect Tim any minute now."

"What a good idea!" exclaimed Mrs. Chisholm. "Oh, Brian, I wish you would stay. The tower room has its own bath. We're having a party on Sunday. Naturally you're invited. An older crowd than you, but Tim will be there, and Gemma—and Gemma's friend Edith Cross. Do stay, Brian. It would be lovely having you here."

He hesitated for a moment. "When does Christine get back?"

"Not for another week or so."

"In that case I'd be delighted to stay. Now I'd better go and cancel my reservation and get my suitcase. I rented a car at the airport."

Without waiting to be asked I handed Mrs. Chisholm a cigarette the second her son had left the room. "Will you let him see you smoke?" I asked.

"In due course. He had to get used to my short hair and painted face." She smiled. "Brian is a very conservative man. I don't want to land too many surprises on him at once."

"If you will excuse me—Helen," (I found her Christian name difficult to say. Although I was immensely flattered that she had asked me to use it, I couldn't help feeling it was a breach of protocol.) "I must go and see about dinner. There are two men to feed, and Tim really likes to chow down."

Downstairs in the kitchen I took out the leg of lamb. It could probably be stretched to serve four, but it would have to be backed up by all sorts of bulky and filling side dishes. I decided to whip up an apple betty, the dessert for people who don't eat dessert. I decided to prepare and bake it now. Just before serving

I would put it back in the oven, already warm from the roast.

There is something unpleasant about coring an apple. You take a specially designed, sharp, circular tool and cut the living centre out of the fruit, leaving only the fleshy skin and moist pulp. The operation is not unlike the one men perform on women who have outgrown their usefulness as breeders. Even more provoking is to realize that when my turn comes I'd rather have the operation performed by a man than a woman. Far better to be treated like an object, a malfunctioning watch or a broken toaster, and to be properly repaired. Men have always treated women like objects, but, I have noticed, it is seldom the beautiful ones who object.

Beautiful women who have some intelligence—and not all of us are bimbos—retaliate by playing the same game with even more skill and manipulating men for their own ends. In case I sound too calculating let me hasten to add that many such relationships turn out to be user friendly. There also have to be trade-offs. The main casualty of realizing that sexual relationships are transactions, like that between salesman and customer, is having to let go the myth of romantic love. Romance sustains itself on the illusion that love is free, just like the million-dollar sweepstake prize offered by certain national magazines to lure subscriptions. Like anything else—pearls, parkas, peanuts—love is a commodity. You get pretty well what you pay for. Romantic love exists in books, in black-and-white movies, in opera. But in that uncomfortable condition known as real life, the only truly romantic love affairs are homosexual.

I am the first to admit that I have probably missed out on a good deal of what women's magazines used to call happiness. That may well be true; but, if so, I have no one to blame but myself. We make our choices, and only a fool or someone on drugs believes the grass is really greener over the fence. My priorities were perfectly straightforward. I wanted security more than I wanted happiness. At the moment I had neither, but I have no one to hold accountable but myself.

No sooner had I put the apple betty into the oven than Brian came into the kitchen. His smile was a shaft of pale sunlight on a snow covered field. "Miss Johnstone, I have to congratulate you. I haven't seen Mother looking as well in a long time. It's more than just cutting her hair and applying makeup; she seems to have undergone a change of attitude. Was it your idea she move downstairs?"

"I have to admit it was. Now she can come down to the ground floor and get out of the house."

"What a difference it has made." He leaned comfortably against the counter and crossed his arms. "When I first moved to Toronto I asked Mother if she wanted to come and live with me, but she didn't want to leave Montreal and her friends. She was determined to remain in this house—she can be very stubborn—and the only way to arrange that was to have Christine come and live with her. Mother has had to make. . ." he paused, searching for the right word, "accommodations in order to live with Christine. I would prefer to see her in a residence, where she could be in contact with other people."

"She may be on the verge of changing her mind." I told him about Mrs. Pitfield coming for dinner and of our visit to Mrs. Potter this morning. "I think your mother was impressed. Give her a bit of time and she may well decide to move."

"It would be a great relief to me if she did."

Using the key hidden in the garage, Tim let himself in through the side door. "Wow! Father!" he exclaimed with evident surprise.

"I was when I got up this morning."

The two men embraced awkwardly, a locker room hug, with no real contact; two amateur actors miming an embrace in a little theatre production.

"Hi, Miss Johnstone," said Tim, smiling as he turned his attention away from his father.

"Your father has been persuaded to stay for the weekend. That will give you two a chance to catch up. Now, if you gentlemen will excuse me, I must go and change. Pale green silk is not ideal for mucking about in the kitchen."

As I spoke I lifted off the unbecoming apron, giving them both a chance to admire the dress to which I had just drawn attention. "Tim, your grandmother is awake, if you'd like to go up and say hello. One last question: does either of you object to garlic?"

The two men looked at one another in evident astonishment, then back at me.

"Not me," said Tim.

"Nor me," echoed his father. "Christine's former cook wouldn't touch garlic with an eleven foot pole."

Having just scored a point, I went upstairs and changed into slacks, a green blouse, and, most importantly, flat shoes. I also slipped on a man's blue shirt, one of several Walter kept at my apartment, folding back the cuffs and turning up the collar to make it seem more blouson, less smock. Finally I checked my makeup and pinned up my hair, twisting it loosely before securing it with a couple of combs. Just before leaving my room I teased out several strands to soften the look.

A sweet disorder in the dress
Kindles in clothes a wantonness.

Contrary to popular belief, opportunity does not always come knocking boldly at the door. More often it announces itself by a faint scratching one must have keen ears to hear. Brian Chisholm was an attractive man, if you happen to like the type. He was successful and single; he did not have two heads or one giant eye in the middle of his forehead. However, Canadian Gothic has never been my style. Although appearances can be deceiving, there was something faintly intimidating about the man. He looked as though he would be right at home in a black frock coat, thumping a Bible and browbeating the gullible for their small, illicit pleasures. Like a good animal he had breeding, but under the veneer of manners, private schools, men's clubs, I suspected there lurked a capacity for ruthlessness. He would never suffer fools or condone weakness.

But, as I took care to remind myself, I had reached an age when I could no longer afford to be choosy—that is unless I wanted to go back to jabbing intravenous needles into reluctant arms and dispensing codeine pills in small paper cups. Brian Chisholm might not be the golden opportunity for which, soaking indolently in scented bathwater, I might have dreamed. But he was the opportunity at hand. My most pressing concern at the moment was to get dinner on the table. This meal would both demonstrate my handiness around the kitchen and satisfy Tim. After checking myself one last time in the mirror, I went downstairs to get started.

I settled down to peel cloves of garlic—one of those pleasant, mindless tasks which occupies the hands and leaves the mind free to wander.

I have never been a serious believer in fate or coincidence. Things either happen or they don't, and to argue the presence of an extrasensory guiding hand strikes me as adolescent. Yet two recent incidents had put me in a reflective mood. The first was the image of myself in the gold lamé gown under an overhead light. Even if I did not look my age, the bloom of youth had definitely faded. How long I would continue to pass for a woman somewhere in her late thirties was hard to predict. Time has a way of cheating cosmetics; and unless a woman is prepared to wear gloves at all times, even in the bath, her hands will sooner or later give her away.

The second sobering event was running into Ian Anderson, if only briefly, at the Ritz. Ian had wanted to marry me, and for a while I seriously considered his proposal. I was younger then, and marriage struck me as a poor deal. Lovers are infinitely more generous than husbands and nothing causes the cash flow to dry up faster than saying "I do." A birthday might occasion a gold bangle, but not a ruby pendant. Last year's fur coat could easily be made over, and a down-filled coat is so much warmer. Instead of high denomination bills dropped into the Lalique vase, I would be reduced to a housekeeping allowance. And for that I must endure the predictable routine of a conjugal bed, as most men will try things with an adventurous woman that they would never dream of attempting with their wives.

Only once did I seriously consider relinquishing my precious freedom. Robert was his name, Robert Beecham; but I called him Bob. He taught an evening course in English literature I decided to take, as on Tuesday evenings the man I was seeing went to his weekly seance. It is difficult to feel serious about a man who, at least once a week, tries to get in touch with the great beyond. But he was rich, and—to use a phrase which might well serve as my epitaph—"His wife didn't understand him."

Professor Beecham and I got to talking one evening after class. I can see him now as a true child of the Sixties, but at the time his tendentious support for a kind of freewheeling search for self-fulfillment was heady stuff. When he argued that "The best lack all conviction, while the worst/Are full of passionate intensity," I sat up straight in my seat and decided that to be both best and full of passionate intensity was indeed a worthy goal. I was not alone.

All the other women taking the course came on to him like wasps at a picnic, but I held back. I was the youngest in the class and in the full flower of my extraordinary beauty. He offered to take me home, and I invited him in for coffee. I didn't even get to plug in the kettle. Sometimes two people simply connect in bed. He had a superb body, a prick as responsive as a tuning fork; and, to borrow the language of pulp fiction, he made me more happy more quickly than any man I have ever known.

Did I really love Bob? Perhaps I did. I certainly did not feel the romantic passion I once felt for my philosophy student. But that kind of amorous intensity lies in the eye of the beholder. It is an invented emotion, a product of the capacity for fiction we all possess to a greater or lesser extent. We fall in love with the clothes, not the emperor. I had once thought myself in heaven; now I knew I was flat on my back on earth.

Hand in hand with sexual energy, as bread to butter or lime with tequila, goes the urge to build a nest, to shut out the world and live out our lives in an eternity of cooing and copulation. I tried to imagine living on a professor's salary and doing without the luxuries I had now come to enjoy. For that kind of high voltage sex I honestly thought I could do it. I also attempted to imagine motherhood, baby food and building blocks. There my conviction faltered, so I put the idea on hold.

What I would have enjoyed, in bed, at breakfast, on weekends, was a man who had all the education I had been denied. Between bouts of lovemaking he would instruct me, guide my reading, channel my intelligence into fertile soil where it would bloom. I had just about convinced myself that marriage was the preferable option when one night, as I lay shuddering in his weightlifter's arms, he asked me to marry him.

By then I had learned to practice guile, not because I wanted to but because I could not otherwise have survived. Most people do not want truth, with its bitter, antiseptic odour. Instead they want illusion, quietly reassuring, softly lit, faintly fragrant. Had I but kept my mouth shut I might at this moment be living on the West Island: aluminum siding, one acre yard, two car garage, gas barbecue, big shaggy dog, impatiens in the shaded flower bed, and children mercifully away at university.

But I was still young enough to believe in truth and the cleansing power of confession. We could not build a marriage on the shifting sands of concealment. So lying there, still flushed from the aftermath of sexual athletics, and about to engage in another bout, I told him my history and how I helped support myself by being accommodating to certain select men.

I felt his body stiffen even as his prick went soft.

"You mean to say you're a prostitute?"

I moved away so our bodies no longer touched. "That's a very uncompromising word. I don't work the sidewalk or make engagements by telephone."

"But you get paid for sex."

"Not quite. I make myself available to men, never more than one at a time, and they in turn help me out with my expenses. There's an element of goodwill. We meet as people, not as hooker and john."

He laughed, a short bark without mirth. "Still, if a man has the money he will find you—'as common as the way between St. Albans and London.'"

"You've lost me."

"It's a line from a play, *Henry IV*, Pistol talking about Doll Tearsheet."

"With a name like that can I conclude she's what you would call a whore."

"You might say."

I pulled the sheet up to my chin. "You astonish me, Bob. What happened to all that liberalism you preached: doing your own thing, letting it all hang out, going with the flow? I have probably slept with fewer men than your swinging secretary who goes out to the singles' bars two or three times a week."

"Yes, but you took money for it."

I could scarcely bring myself to believe that the man lying rigid beside me was the same liberal professor who in the class-room always seemed to have a scrap of Yeats, or a couplet from Wordsworth, or lines from Shakespeare to underline his unconventional and highly permissive ideas.

"You must have realized you were not the first man I have slept with."

"I did, but I had no idea you were turning tricks to pay the rent." He slid out of bed and began to pull on his clothes.

"Tell me something, Bob. Is it the money that is really

bothering you, or the fact that I was calling the shots? I performed a service, on my terms, and got paid for it. I did not demand fidelity and commitment and tenderness and help with the dishes. But that doesn't mean I don't have them to offer."

By now he was almost dressed. "I guess it boils down to a question of experience. You've had more than I want in a wife."

"Has it ever occurred to you that in any other area you'd run from inexperience? If you were to have your appendix removed, wouldn't you prefer a seasoned surgeon? Would you go to a student dentist for a gold crown? Yet you run away from a woman who's experienced in making love as though she were a—a . . ."

"Whore?"

Stung, I flushed with the quick anger of wounded candour. "That shouldn't be a problem. You're inexperienced enough for both of us."

I could see I had touched a nerve. "Goodbye, Gemma. I hope things work out for you." He pulled on his corduroy jacket and left.

I seldom cry, but I did then, abandoning myself luxuriously to grief. When is love ever sweeter than after it has just ended? I had been proposed to and jilted in a matter of minutes. My vanity had taken a bruising; so had my ego. I washed them both in tears.

After a while I dried my eyes, took a long hot shower, and made a pot of tea. As I stirred the leaves I realized there is wisdom in old saws. The truth really had set me free.

That night the wife of my current admirer burned his Ouija board in the fireplace and shouted that she could no longer live with a man who wanted to communicate with the dead. The resulting divorce put an end to our liaison, for he feared that once he was free I would want to snap him up. But by then I had met a French-Canadian who held an important job with the *Caisses de dépot*, a kind of do-it-yourself bank indigenous to the Province of Quebec. By the time the investigators had tracked him down he had embezzled enough funds to buy me a Matisse drawing. I wrote to him in prison for a while, but he kept insisting I return the drawing. One day I discovered I had mislaid his address.

My time with Bob had been too brief to leave much of a trace. Unlike the last five minutes of a TV movie-of-the-week he did not begin to hang around my doorstep, saying he understood and begging me to forgive him and reconsider. I heard he finished his Ph.D. and took a teaching position out West. I never saw him again.

What I did manage to salvage, along with odds of Yeats and ends of Eliot, was the memory of an intense sexuality, bright as crystal yet warm as cashmere. I understood I would probably never know that kind of intense physical happiness again. And I never have.

Nine

Once I had finished peeling the surface tissue, I cut the ivory garlic cloves into slices. With the knife I made a series of parallel cuts along the top and sides of the lamb. Into each I tucked a sliver of garlic. Once the apple betty had cooked, I slid the roast into a 350° oven.

I was washing and tearing lettuce for salad when Tim came into the kitchen. "Gran suggested I come down to see if you need help with dinner. Can I set the table?"

I smiled inwardly at the thought of this young giant setting out place mats and teaspoons. I knew I was being sexist, but the fact remains that I am an unregenerate sexist. Girls set the table; boys change flat tires. Girls have pinking shears; boys have pliers. Girls pee sitting down; boys pee standing up. I suppose that kind of thinking makes me a dinosaur. At least I am a size 14 dinosaur with decent skin.

"Perhaps you could check that there is beer in the fridge. You and your father might like one with dinner. Or does he drink wine?"

"Father doesn't drink much of anything. A scotch and water or two." Tim laughed engagingly. "I like taking him out to dinner when he's in town: one drink, one entrée. And I earn merit points for picking up the tab."

While Tim stocked the refrigerator with beer, I searched the bar for white vermouth. I poured one-and-a-half cups into a small heavy saucepan and brought it to a boil.

Tim came to stand at my elbow. He made me feel like Alice in Wonderland after she has eaten the mushroom. "What's that?"

"It will turn into sauce for the pasta I will serve. The principal ingredients are vermouth and Gorgonzola."

"Wow! Sounds good. I was getting pretty tired of fast food and frozen dinners zapped in the microwave."

"This weekend you'll be living high off the hog. Did you finish reading *Tom Jones?*"

"Yes. It wasn't easy, but I did it. I guess we've become so used to the author keeping himself in the background that it's disturbing to be addressed directly by him." He opened a can of beer and crossed to sit at the table.

"Isn't it just another way of telling a story?" I started washing lettuce while keeping an eye on the simmering vermouth. "Some authors write mostly in dialogue; others from several points of view. Some writers know everything about their characters, or else tell the story from a narrow focus. I don't remember that I minded the presence of the author. But it's a long time since I read *Tom Jones.*"

Tim weighed what I had said. "I suppose you're right. It is only a mode of writing fiction, and just as legitimate as any other. Perhaps the novel is being adversely affected by television. We want things short, vivid, punchy. The author chatting at length to the reader as himself slows down the pace and diverts us from the plot."

"Have you read *Clarissa Harlowe* for your course?"

"I'm trying to. I have to admit that compared to *Clarissa, Tom*

Jones is a breeze, almost like a detective story."

"I had trouble with *Clarissa*, even in the Modern Library abridged version. I found it a profoundly unpleasant book. Prurient is the word that comes to mind. All that intense preoccupation with one lay. And she is so vapid. I can't imagine Lovelace would go to all that bother. I realize Clarissa's whole identity is tied up with her concept of chastity. My own bias intrudes, but I find her preoccupation with chastity far more difficult to accept than, for instance, the author popping up from time to time to address the reader directly."

By now the vermouth had been reduced to about one half. I added two cups of heavy cream, brought the mixture back to a boil, and reduced the heat. While it simmered I added freshly ground black pepper and a pinch of nutmeg.

"Where did you study English, Miss Johnstone?"

"I never studied formally. I wanted very much to take a liberal arts degree, but the money just wasn't there, and I had to earn a living. So I went from high school into nursing."

"How did you come to read those books? I mean nobody reads eighteenth-century novels if not for a course."

I stirred the mixture on the stove before transferring it to a double boiler. "I was curious, I suppose. I borrowed reading lists from a friend. She did the course with Cole's notes, but I read the books: *Moll Flanders*, *Humphry Clinker*, *Tristram Shandy*—I loved that book. I've always wanted to read it again. It seemed so contemporary."

I measured oil into a small jar for salad dressing. "You're fortunate to be reading those books now. Long novels, serious long novels, require time; and the older you get the less willing you are to make that kind of long-term commitment. At your age you have all the time in the world. At mine, well . . ." I broke off. Unwilling to complete the thought I made rather a show of opening the oven door and checking the roast.

I turned down the heat under the double boiler. "Now I'd better go up and see if your grandmother needs anything." I smiled. "We can deal with the nineteenth century over dinner."

The door to Mrs. Chisholm's room stood ajar. I knocked. "May I come in?"

"By all means," she called out. "Brian and I are just having a visit."

"Would you like me to come back in a few minutes?"

"Not at all." Mrs. Chisholm waved me inside. "Gemma is practically one of the family."

Brian turned to give me a wintry smile. I raised my head slightly and opened my eyes wide, so wide that the irises were completely surrounded by white, throwing the green into sharp relief. The glance lasted only a second, and I looked away first. But the message had been clear: green eyes, green light.

"Now, Brian, what were you saying? But first, I must have a cigarette." She smiled at her son. "Yes, I have succumbed. I am smoking again, and loving it." She inhaled blissfully, exhaled, and sat up straight. "All right. I'm listening."

"Mother, you know what the doctor said about smoking."

"Yes, Brian, but the doctor is not a deity. Just remember: many doctors graduate with a B average. And next to the ministry they are the biggest naysayers in the world. Now what was it you wanted to ask me?"

Brian sat playing with a ballpoint pen, repeatedly pushing the button to advance and retract the tip. I could tell he would have preferred me not to be present, but it was his mother's room and she had asked me to stay.

"I've been doing a little investigating, Mother, and I think it would be a good idea if you were to incorporate yourself as a private company. That way you will not have to pay so much inheritance tax."

Mrs. Chisholm took a second reflective pull on her cigarette. "Once I am dead, Brian, I won't have to pay a penny in inheritance tax. You will."

"Only a manner of speaking, Mother. I was referring to your estate."

"A most unfortunate manner of speaking. I am not dead yet. And now with Gemma to take care of me I may well live to be a hundred."

Brian turned to give me another chilly smile. I smiled back. Like a TV talk show hostess I made apples of my cheeks. "We're all indebted to Miss Johnstone for that," he said. "But," the smile faded, "the U.S. government is now imposing a hefty inheritance tax on U.S. holdings owned by Canadian citizens."

"Dead Canadian citizens," added Mrs. Chisholm.

"Yes, Mother, but you have to admit that once we—we lose you, then incorporation becomes impossible."

Mrs. Chisholm stiffened her spine. "You lose car keys, Brian, not parents. And I admit nothing. Incorporation indeed. You make me sound like Exxon."

"Mother, do be reasonable." Brian leaned forward. "This incorporation will not really affect you. It is just a legal formality which will make settling your estate just that much easier for the heirs."

"How can you be so certain it won't affect me?" demanded his mother. "My hearing might not be what it once was, but I am not hard of thinking. There will be legal fees for the incorporation.

As a private company will I be required to pay more income tax than as a private citizen? What about the carrying charges?"

"Why don't you let me make some inquiries? If we find the move to be in everybody's best interest, we can proceed. You will have no bother whatsoever. With the power of attorney Christine can act in your place and you won't have to worry about a thing."

"I am going to revoke the power of attorney. The document is being prepared even as we speak. I will sign it Monday morning."

"I see." Brian stood. "Well, Mother, it was just a thought. May I make myself a drink?"

"Of course. Gemma will bring me downstairs in a few minutes."

With a small, stiff bow he left the room. In the eddy of silence Mrs. Chisholm butted out her cigarette.

"Do you know, Gemma, if two weeks ago he had suggested I incorporate myself I would meekly have acquiesced. Had he come up to the tower room where I sat in bed, my hair in braids, my face innocent of makeup, I would have agreed to his proposal. To be fair to Brian, he is not aggressive like his sister, but he is a man. Moreover, he is a successful one. Who am I, his mere mother, to contradict him—but I did!"

"I think a good deal of self-assurance has to do with good grooming. Would you like to wear your burgundy robe for dinner?"

Mrs. Chisholm nodded.

"To look your best is more than a question of vanity; it is a defense against the world. I am convinced that well turned out women are assaulted less frequently than those who let their appearance slide. If you don't look like a victim you are less likely to become one."

Mrs. Chisholm reached out and took my hand. "If it weren't for you I wouldn't have had the courage to say no. Before you came I looked like a victim, and was treated like one." She got to her feet with determination. "How does that song go? 'There'll be some changes made today. There'll be some changes made!' And I'm darned if at my age I'm going to become a corporation."

"My mother—the corporation."

We both started to giggle, and we were both still giggling as I left the room with a promise to return shortly to bring her downstairs.

I put a large pot of water onto the burner and turned the heat up high. Into the sauce slowly thickening in the double boiler I stirred in crumbled Gorgonzola and grated Parmesan. As I set the table I wondered whether I had been imprudent to remain in the room while Brian tried to persuade his mother to incorporate herself. He could well resent my having seen him bested by his mother. Male chauvinists of a certain type are as easy to spot as postmen or public security officers. They all wear a uniform, in Brian's case a dark suit of ultra-conservative cut. That Brian Chisholm was a chauvinist *pure laine*, as they say in Quebec, I had not the slightest doubt. Ordinarily that particular attitude did not present a problem, for me at least. Under normal circumstances I can deal readily with right-wing men by playing up to their cast concrete conceptions of how a woman should behave. She must never push, only tug gently. She must never be seen as bold or forward, but always patient, passive, pliant, waiting for the man to make the first move. Unfortunately the whole process takes time, more time than I had at the moment.

As I set out the solid, sincere, asymmetrical salt and pepper shakers, probably made by one of the children at craft camp, I wondered whether I should seat myself above or below the salt. Time was when salt served to separate the upper from the lower classes. Nowadays it is only the lower classes who use it.

As I intended to serve the pilaff with the lamb, I took a handful of uncooked spaghetti and broke it into one-inch pieces, enough to fill about half a cup. Using powdered chicken stock I made two cups of soup, measuring the ingredients into a jar and shaking vigorously. Into a bowl I measured two cups of long grained rice. By now the water had come to a boil, so I added the tortellini and turned the heat to medium.

There being nothing further to do at the moment, I went upstairs to fetch Mrs. Chisholm so I could settle her at the table with a sherry and a cigarette while I continued my preparations.

"Gemma, I just realized we have people coming to the house on Sunday; we have a caterer, and a bartender, but I have no idea what I am going to wear."

"What about your burgundy robe?"

"I'd like to wear something that doesn't look quite so much like a dressing gown."

"I see. The other morning, when I was looking for your gray wool, I found a closet full of evening clothes. I assumed from the size they were yours."

"Mementoes of a misspent youth. When I think of all the parties I went to, and the balls. I must have been a very frivolous young woman."

"Or a very sensible one. Who wouldn't go to a ball, given the chance? Which of us hasn't dreamed of being Cinderella, of going to a wonderful party looking our best and meeting the man of our dreams—falling in love as we waltzed. As for the pumpkin, the mice, the ashes, they serve to remind us we must return to daily life. We all have to deal with the ashes, one way or another. But once in a while we can escape into a state of heightened awareness and have a ball."

"You speak as one who has never been to a ball. They are not nearly so glamorous as you imagine. I think the main problem was our shoes. Can you imagine dancing all night in glass slippers? They may look charming, but they are very hard on the feet." Mrs. Chisholm laughed. "And with a transparent shoe you can- not wear arch supports. Furthermore, the men who were really good dancers, our Princes Charming for the evening, were rarely promising marriage prospects. I can remember a whole group of elegant young men I saw only at dances. It was as if they had no existence away from the ballroom; no everyday clothes, only tails. I wonder where they all went."

"I would hazard a guess you would find them in Anglo- Catholic churches or in Key West. But to return to your original question, surely there must be something upstairs you could wear. Tell you what. Why don't I go up and have a look after dinner. I'll bring down whatever might be suitable, and we can decide."

"Don't you think a long skirt might be a bit overpowering for a noon party?"

"At your age, Helen, you don't follow fashion; you establish it. Are you ready to go downstairs?"

After settling Mrs. Chisholm at one end of the table with her nightly sherry, inevitable cigarette, and a magazine, I dropped about one third of a stick of butter into a medium saucepan to melt. Once it started to bubble I added the spaghetti bits, stirring constantly until they had turned golden brown. When they were just the right shade of ochre I added the chicken stock. While it came to a boil I washed the rice under hot running water until all cloudiness had gone and the water ran clear. As soon as the chicken stock started to boil I added the rice, stirred it once, covered the pan, and turned the heat down low. I know rice and tortellini at the same meal were a bit stodgy, but they would help to fill up Tim.

While I performed my sleight of hand at the stove, I remembered an admirer, now long gone, who liked to steal up behind me when I was involved with a tricky bit of preparation, like stirring lemon juice into hollandaise sauce or watching eggs turn just the right consistency to fold into an omelette. He would slip it in through the back door and try to make me screw up, in a manner of speaking. It was less a case of sex at the stove than a war of wills. Could he break my concentration? Would the hollandaise separate or the eggs overcook?

He never succeeded, simply because my concentration was more focussed than his. After a while he began to think with his prick rather than his brain. I would continue to stir in regular, rhythmic strokes while he panted and heaved as I folded the omelette, or tested the broccoli with a fork to see if it was cooked. Sliding an omelette onto a platter while your lunch companion is having his magic moment adds a whole new dimension to grace under pressure.

I was relieved that Mrs. Chisholm, preoccupied with her cigarette and the magazine, couldn't read my thoughts.

When the tortellini had cooked *al dente*, I drained and rinsed it, returned the pasta to the pot, and stirred in the gorgonzola sauce.

I found the two men in the den watching TV. "Grub's up in the kitchen, gentlemen," I said from the door.

"Suits me," said Tim, getting instantly to his feet.

Brian merely smiled. I suppose even that was a concession, but I would have given not a little to know if there was anything that really turned him on.

The tortellini with Gorgonzola was pronounced a success. We all ate our first helpings and Tim polished off what was left. By now the pilaff had cooked and the roast of lamb sat on a platter waiting to be carved. The kitchen was heavy with the fragrance of cooked food, with just an acrid hint from the cigarette Mrs. Chisholm liked to smoke between courses.

Mrs. Chisholm wore her contentment like a friendly cardigan. Freshly made up, her hair stylishly cut, wearing a handsome robe, she sat at her own table smoking a cigarette, flanked by the two most important men in her life. Tim sat quietly, his immense hands resting on his place mat, waiting for the next plate of food with an almost monastic concentration. I enjoyed seeing him eat with such evident relish, even though it was his father I hoped to impress.

Mrs. Chisholm's smoking gave me just the delay I needed to make a sauce for the lamb. (Gravy is for boarding schools.) I put the roasting pan onto a hot burner and stirred in about a cup of beef broth and half a cup of white vermouth, with just enough cornstarch to thicken slightly. When it was hot I ladled it into a bowl. Then, with just the right amount of deference, I asked Brian (Mr. Chisholm to his face) if he would mind carving. He would be glad to, even though a little out of practice. I suggested carving was a skill which, like riding a bicycle, one never really lost. We laughed, not because I had been amusing but from a feeling of shared goodwill. Good food has a way of melting barriers.

Much information can be conveyed without speech. I served the pilaff onto plates which I brought to Brian so he could lay out slices of lamb, carved with the skill of a surgeon. I smiled my appreciation, brushing against him as if by accident. He appeared not to notice. If only I could push the right button I suspected I would unleash an intense if repressed sexuality. Once I had found the right button I was home free; but, like someone learning to use a computer, I hadn't quite got the knack.

The lamb, with its savour of garlic, was declared succulent, the sauce delicious, the pilaff interesting. When one is accustomed to badly cooked food, anything novel, even if well prepared, becomes a little suspect. Except for Tim; his appreciation translated itself into a large second helping. We drank a red wine, one that had the modest distinction of having been bottled in France and not imported in bulk to be decanted here. Although I spoke little, I managed to maintain my presence, passing the sauce, offering mint sauce as an alternative—happily refused. I volunteered second helpings. Other times I remained perfectly still, scarcely breathing, until my very immobility drew attention; at which point I moved my fork or dabbed at the corners of my mouth with a napkin. The whole understated performance was designed to keep me in the forefront of Brian's attention.

By the time I had cleared away the salad course everyone had eaten enough. Only Tim remained game for the apple betty, now warming in the oven. I explained that in deference to his distaste for desserts I had made a concoction of fruit and dough, substituting lemon juice for sugar. He gave me a smile, radiating all the warmth his father lacked, and agreed to try a slice, refusing a serving of ice cream on the side. I couldn't blame him. Ice cream is a truly unpleasant substance, cold, sticky, sweet. When I was a child, Mother was convinced that if I ate ice cream that wasn't made at home I would come down with infantile paralysis. As she could never be bothered to make the frozen concoction, I never developed the taste for it.

While Tim quietly ate a second serving of dessert, I offered coffee, refused by all as being too stimulating this late in the day. Tim and his father went off to bond in front of the television set, while Mrs. Chisholm opted to smoke while I cleared up.

It had been pretty good food, if heavy on the starches. However, one cannot satisfy a trencherman like Tim with *cuisine minceur*. Also it is the custom of North Americans to applaud. Success is easier to deal with than failure. Achievement makes no claim on pity or tact, and congratulations are easier to utter than condolences. The important fallout from dinner lay in my having convinced Brian I knew my way around a kitchen. Sexual attraction comes and goes, but cooking is forever.

"You continue to astonish me, Gemma." Mrs. Chisholm poured herself half a glass of wine. "You make it all seem so effortless. Whenever Christine cooks, which isn't too often, believe me, she turns preparing even a simple meal into one of the labours of Hercules. I wish to heaven Brian would marry someone like you. He is too old to figure in a Jane Austen novel, but he is sorely 'in want of a wife.'"

I laughed, a bit self-consciously. "I suppose Brian is the best judge of that. And," this time my smile was genuine, "the best thing about marrying him would be to gain you as a mother-in-law."

Mrs. Chisholm made a gesture of dismissal. "It's lovely of you to say so, even if it isn't true."

By now the dishwasher was ready to go. I pushed the switch

on that most brilliant of labour saving devices and joined Mrs. Chisholm at the table.

"Whenever you're ready I'll take you upstairs. Then I can go and check through the gowns for something you can wear on Sunday."

"I still wonder about a long skirt for a noon party."

"With a long skirt you won't have to wear pantyhose, only knee length stockings."

Mrs. Chisholm laughed. "But of course! Whatever would I do without you? Shall we go up?"

"Would you like to join the men for a little TV?"

"That might be pleasant."

The two of us made our way to the den, where Tim and his father were watching a documentary on the American Civil War. Our entrance caused a bit of a stir. Chairs were shifted, a place made.

"I'll be on the top floor if you need anything," I said to Mrs. Chisholm, at the same time flashing Brian my wide-open-eyed look. I hoped that with Tim to keep his grandmother company Brian might find an excuse to go up to his room, giving us a chance to talk.

On my way upstairs I ducked into my own bedroom to check out my hair and make-up, before continuing up to the third floor and into the bedroom where the gowns were hung. Most of them were cut to expose the neck and shoulders, evidence of that curious custom which obliges men to encase themselves on formal occasions while women take it all off, at least down to the waist.

I lifted out a hanger, put it back, lifted out another. This gown was a definite possibility: a stocking dress in black silk jersey gathered around a seam running right down the front, trimmed in gold braid. Its long fitted sleeves had wide gold cuffs trimmed in the same gold braid. The main drawback was the plunging neckline, although perhaps I could improvise something, a bit of fabric or a brooch to make the *décolletage* less alarming. I laid the gown across the bed and continued my search.

After several more forays I lifted out a beautiful ivory brocade robe with a high neck and long sleeves trimmed in mink. A beautiful garment, its sleeves and yoke were cut from the same piece of fabric. The mink trim looked a bit tired, but it could be brushed up. Long sleeves and a long skirt cover a multitude of sins, so I laid out the gown beside the black jersey.

At that moment I heard the stairs creak, indicating someone was coming up. I assumed a thoughtful, graceful pose, my left arm folded across my abdomen, supporting my right arm and hand on which I rested my chin. A figure blocked the doorway, and I looked up to see Tim.

"Are you going to wear the gold dress again?"

"Not at the moment." I smiled in spite of myself. "I'm trying to pick a gown for your grandmother to wear to her party. As long as you're here, why don't you give me an opinion?"

I picked up the black jersey and held it against myself, while Tim looked at it thoughtfully. Then I held up the ivory brocade.

"If you were choosing it for yourself," he said after a pause, "I'd take the black. It would suit you. But I think the off-white is better for Gran. It's almost the same colour as her hair. And the black is too," he paused for a word, "too young."

"I tend to agree with you," I said as I covered the black dress with its protective bag and returned it to the closet. "Aren't you interested in the Civil War?"

"Yes, but not in a series of stills with voice-over. Also Father was beginning to do a number. He wonders if I shouldn't take an M.B.A., either before or after going to law school."

"It doesn't sound like a bad idea, except that it means a lot more studying for you." I picked up the ivory gown and draped it over my arm.

"It's not the studying I mind. . ." Tim sat heavily on the edge of the bed which groaned under his bulk. "The problem is that I don't much want to go to law school in the first place. What I'd really like to do is take an M.A. in English and History, then a Ph.D. I'd rather be a teacher than a lawyer, but Father won't hear of it."

"I suspect your father is a conservative man." I was treading softly. "He understands that as a lawyer, or an entrepreneur, you will earn a better living than as an academic. I am certain he wants what is best for you."

"True, but on his terms. He'd far rather see me as a CEO than as dean of a faculty."

"Perhaps. And the only advice I have to offer sounds like a tired truism: it is your life and you must live it as you see best. May I add one word of caution, without sounding like the enemy?"

Tim proferred his engaging smile. "Yes, please."

"When you're in your twenties money doesn't seem very important. You have youth and vitality. You can work hard and play hard and go without sleep, and still operate full steam ahead. The world is your oyster, if you happen to like oysters. As you get older, however, the energy begins to dwindle. Creature comforts become more important, and they cost. Again that is a decision you must make for yourself."

"I won't have to worry on that score. It's no secret that Gran is leaving her money in trust to the grandchildren, and I hope it's many years before she dies. But Father and I don't see eye to eye on money. He doesn't consider it something to use to buy goods, cars or stereos. He will buy services, hotels, restaurant meals, if he can write them off as business expenses. Money for him is an almost abstract substance, like wheat or oil. It is to be manipulated, not spent. He keeps me on a tight allowance because it's good for my character to be frugal and to develop a habit of hard work. If I am to be successful it must be on his terms, taking whatever money I may have and using it to make more money. He would never understand my wanting to live off the money I have so I can do something I enjoy. I see two hundred dollars as one hell of a weekend. He would prefer to see me study and put the money in the bank. I would find his attitude easier to understand if he were a self-made man; he earned it so he wants to keep it. But Father has never been poor. Yet he seems to think that keeping me on a strict allowance will fill me with the desire to get out there and earn a fortune for myself."

"Tim," I said, brushing the mink trim with the back of my hand, "I can only repeat what I have already said. The one person you have to live with twenty-four hours a day is yourself. Remember that. Also, discontent has a way of showing. If you are not happy with yourself you will not develop into a pleasant person to be around. God knows, life is not a popularity contest; but your work, whatever it is, will occupy the major part of your life. Why start out with the handicap of a profession you don't want to pursue?"

I smiled. "And now I think I'd better go down and check on your grandmother. She's had a lot of excitement today, and stimulation can be more tiring than activity."

"Miss Johnstone?"

I stopped in the doorway and turned. "Yes?"

"Thanks for hearing me out."

"Advice is cheap, Tim. And the lovely thing about telling someone what to do is that it makes you feel very wise and in control of your life. It is I who should thank you."

It was a pretty good exit line, even if I had to throw it away on Tim. I would have much preferred Brian to follow me upstairs, although my common sense told me he was not the kind of man to go trailing around after the help. If I could only find the right button, and I had better find it before he returned to Toronto on Sunday afternoon.

By the time I went downstairs, Mrs. Chisholm was ready to retire. "Such a worthy documentary," she said as we went slowly up the stairs, "and such heavy going. I have reached the age when I want to be entertained, not instructed."

"I'm afraid my idea of the Civil War is *Gone With the Wind*. We paused for a moment on the landing. "Although it's just about time for a revisionist miniseries, one that makes President Lincoln into a whiskey guzzling womanizer reading the Gettysburg Address from cue cards. 'Brought to you by the makers of Drain-O, for a lovelier complexion. She's engaged; she's lovely; she uses Drain-O.'"

Mrs. Chisholm paused to laugh. "Now that one I would stay up to watch."

We entered the bedroom where I had laid the ivory brocade across the bed.

"My ivory brocade!" she exclaimed. "I had quite forgotten it. I can still remember how furious my husband was when he learned how much it had cost, even though it was my money. To think I shall wear it again after all these years."

"Would you like to try it on, just to make sure?"

"Possibly a good idea." I helped her into the gown and fastened it up the back. As she turned to study herself in the mirror, a subtle change took place. Although still the same old lady I had helped to dress, she seemed to swell. She stood tall, confronting the mirror with a newfound authority. It was almost as if the garment threw down a challenge, silent but real, and Helen Chisholm rose to meet it. Even her hair, now short and close to her head, was the right style for the gown.

She stood under the overhead light with the assurance that springs from feeling comfortable about her age. Nothing suggested she wanted to subtract years, whereas I would have given not a little to have been able to carry off the gold lamé. Maybe the time would come when, like Mrs. Chisholm, I too would no longer quail before my reflection. But enough of my beauty remained to make me want to cling to what I had. Knowing that countless other women have confronted the same dilemma did not make the truth easier for me. There are times when even intelligence lets us down.

After I got Mrs. Chisholm settled in bed, both Tim and Brian looked in to say goodnight. Brian pleaded work and continued on up to his room, while Tim went down to watch something on TV filled with the sound of car chases and semi-automatic weapons.

In my own room I undressed quickly and pulled on my nightgown and matching *peignoir*. As Gerry had suggested, I looked not unlike the personification of a Greek virtue, but the pale green ensemble showed my bust to be still high and firm. My plan was to visit Brian in his room on some pretext or other and to send out an erotic message. The problem was that I did not feel a strong physical attraction for Brian, and this was not a time for the bumping, grinding, hip swinging kind of obvious sexual advance. Genuine desire does have a way of making itself felt. If only I could chat myself up, turn myself on as it were, so that I would send out the right signals.

A sudden inspiration made me open my bag and take out the money I had withdrawn from the bank. A taupe hundred dollar bill remained along with some crimson fifties. As I fingered them lovingly I began, almost imperceptibly at first, to feel that reassuring itch. Were Brian to volunteer a scratch, I might just be tempted.

Returning the money to my purse, I climbed the stairs to find a hem of light visible under the door of the tower room. Hesitating for just a second, I went up to the door and knocked.

"Come in."

Slowly I opened the door to reveal myself, draped, flowing, available. Brian, his shirt unbuttoned at the neck, looked up from the brimming briefcase on his knees. "Yes, Miss Johnstone?" His glance registered my presence, nothing more.

"Before I turn in, I was wondering if there was anything you would like. A glass of milk? Tea? A highball?"

"Nothing at the moment, thank you. Goodnight."

"Well, goodnight," I echoed lamely, his evident indifference pushing me through the door, which I closed as slowly as I could. Even after I heard the latch click I paused, hoping for an "Oh, Miss Johnstone," followed by a request. But the silence positively shrieked.

I took some slight comfort in imagining that with both his mother and his son in the house, Brian would be reluctant to come on to the housekeeper/companion. But a nurse in a white starched uniform is one thing, a beautiful redhead in a fitted nightgown another.

Cross and disgruntled, I returned to my room and picked up a detective novel, one of those with a corpse on page three and the tacit assumption that finding the killer really matters. In minutes my eyelids began to droop. I climbed into bed and switched off the light. After a good night's sleep, anything was possible. Tomorrow I would move mountains, or at the very least get Brian Chisholm to drop his guard.

Ten

aturday morning got off to an early start. I had just finished dressing when I heard someone coming down from the third floor. As I came out of my room I met Brian, fully dressed, on his way to the kitchen. We greeted each other soundlessly, and I followed him downstairs.

While he picked up the paper at the front door, I started the coffee machine.

"I would prefer tea, Miss Johnstone, if you wouldn't mind." He disappeared behind the *Gazette*. I plugged in the kettle and began to organize breakfast.

Brian's demands were modest, one three-minute egg and two slices of whole wheat toast without butter. Comfortable in the slacks I had worn to prepare dinner, I was just as glad I had decided against trailing downstairs in my *peignoir*. If it hadn't triggered a reaction last night at his bedroom door, it could hardly be expected to compete with editorials and a runny yolk.

Once the coffee was ready I carried a cup upstairs to Mrs. Chisholm, but she was still half asleep. She must have been tired from the cumulative effect of an uncharacteristically busy week. Back in the kitchen, Brian had finished his breakfast. Fitting the sections of the paper neatly together, he folded it in half, then in half again.

"Miss Johnstone, I'm planning to take Mother and Tim out for dinner tonight. I know you will have to prepare for the party tomorrow, which means you won't have to cook dinner."

"That's very thoughtful of you, Mr. Chisholm, but I am quite well organized. The party is being catered, and the cleaning woman comes today. It would be no trouble at all for me to prepare dinner, I assure you."

I meant what I said. In spite of his indifference so far, I had not given up on Brian Chisholm. However, I needed to have him around so I could convince him beyond all doubt that this excellent cook and competent organizer was also, given half a chance, a veritable goddess of love, or at least good value in the feathers. Were he to head off to a restaurant he would be out of my orbit. It was to my distinct advantage to cook him dinner here.

"Why don't we see how Mother feels about it? I'll just go up and have a word with her before I leave. I will be out for lunch. Thank you for breakfast, Miss Johnstone." And he was gone. No smile, no lingering look, no backward glance. Now you see him; now you don't. It was all I could do not to take his dirty plate and slam it onto the floor.

Strategy, however, seemed more productive than picking up shards of china. Perhaps I had to make Brian see me as more than just an adjunct to his mother. Tomorrow's party could well give me the opportunity to present myself as hostess rather than mere companion. If so, I would have to look the part. The dress I wanted was at my apartment. Maybe I would ask Tim to drive me down to pick it up, once he had surfaced.

Partially consoled, I poached Mrs. Chisholm an egg, sprinkling the yolk with a little paprika, more for appearance than flavour, and carried it upstairs.

"Brian has just made the most delightful suggestion," she began as I came through the door. "He is going to take me out for dinner tonight, along with Tim, if he wants to come. I can't honestly remember the last time I went out for dinner."

"Are you sure you won't be overdoing it?" I asked as I positioned the tray. "Tomorrow will be a big day, and I don't want you to get overtired."

"Don't worry. We won't be late. Brian suggested we go early, so as to avoid the Saturday night crush. And it means you won't have to cook a meal."

"I really don't mind in the least," I said sourly. "I have the menu planned."

"We can have your meal Sunday night, or Monday. And since we have no other outing planned for today, I really would like to have dinner somewhere with Brian."

I nodded. To remind myself I was being paid to look after the mother, not to put the make on her son, did little to sweeten my disposition. I returned grumpily to the kitchen to thumb my cross way through the newspaper.

The bell to the kitchen door gave two short rings. I crossed to admit Louise, dressed much as she had been yesterday, with the exception of a pair of dark glasses, unnecessary as the day was overcast. A closer look showed me that even the opaque surface of the lens could not fully conceal the bruise that surrounded her left eye.

We exchanged good mornings, and I poured her a cup of coffee. She looked as if she could use it.

"Will you be able to work?" I asked, signalling I had seen the bruise but was keeping my distance.

"Yes," she replied without elaboration.

"If you don't feel up to it, Fran and I can manage."

"I'll be okay," she insisted, and began to weep silently.

I busied myself around the kitchen, doing nothing in particular, until the soundless crisis had passed.

"You barely know me," I began, "and it's none of my business, but if you want to talk I'm prepared to listen."

"There's not much to tell," she said as she dug a Kleenex from her bag. "The man I live with is out of work. He wanted me to hand over the money I earned yesterday, and when I refused he hit me."

"Does this happen often?"

"No, this was the first time. And it will be the last," she announced with some spirit. "I would have left on the spot, but I have a daughter, and I didn't think I could yank her out of the only home she knows."

"In other words, you have no place to go."

"No."

"How old is she?"

"Eighteen."

"Are you concerned about leaving her alone with him?"

"Yes and no. I don't really think he'd hurt her, but she saw it happen. She might say something that could set him off. I hope she'll be okay. I had to come to work. I need the money."

"Have some more coffee," I said. "I won't be long."

I went quickly upstairs, ostensibly to collect Mrs. Chisholm's breakfast tray, but I had another, urgent motive. To see Louise's bruised face caused time to fold in on itself. As vividly as if it were last night, I remembered my own mother and how she had looked after Father knocked her around. Poor Mother, pretty in that English tea rose fashion, her flawless skin angry red from slaps or stained with bruises; always convinced she was somehow to blame for his rages. That early experience convinced me violence is the ultimate obscenity and must be opposed in any way possible. I intended to meddle.

"Did I hear the bell?" asked Mrs. Chisholm as I came into the room.

"Yes, Louise is here." I dropped my voice even though there was no one to overhear. "Try to ignore the dark glasses. The man she is living with beat her up and she has a badly bruised eye."

Mrs. Chisholm went rigid in her chair. "He did what?"

"He slapped her around, pretty badly it would seem. She wouldn't hand over her pay."

"I don't believe what you are saying. I know women do get beaten up, but not any women we know. What is she going to do? Has she called the police?"

"No, it's the first time he's struck her. And you know what the police are like. Perhaps you don't. They would be less than sympathetic towards an Indian woman living common law. She has nowhere else to go right now. And she has an eighteen year old daughter; otherwise she would have left on the spot."

Mrs. Chisholm folded her hands in her lap and sat up straight. Her position suggested she was going to make a pronouncement *ex cathedra*.

"She must remain here. And her daughter must come to stay too. There are four empty rooms upstairs. She cannot remain under the same roof with a man who has beaten her."

"I know Tim won't mind," I said, covering all bases, "but what about Mr. Chisholm?"

"Why should he mind? He's way up there in the tower room, with his own bath. And if he does mind he can go off to his hotel. It is my house after all."

I picked up the tray. "If you're quite certain . . . I'll go and tell Louise. I know she will be very pleased. She'll probably come up and have a word with you herself."

"I should be glad to see her."

As I went downstairs I hoped the Big Person in the sky would forgive me for my guile, as it had been devoid of self-interest.

Louise was just organizing herself to go to work. God bless cleaning women; they bring a new high gloss to old clichés. I had been able to say to Louise's predecessor, "You're fired!" Now I was able to say to Louise, "Sit down. I have something to tell you."

At first she was stunned, as if the possibility of shelter for both herself and her daughter could hardly be imagined, let alone realized. Then she started to thank me.

"Save your thanks for Mrs. Chisholm," I suggested. "It is her house after all."

For the first time this morning Louise smiled. "Yes, but you put her up to it."

"The facts speak for themselves. Now, we have to get your daughter safely over here. What's her name?"

"Claire."

"Why don't I telephone. Then if he answers he won't recognize my voice."

"I have to hand it to you, Gemma, you know how to cover your . . ."

"Ass?"

We both laughed. I dialled Louise's number, and the voice of a young woman said, "Hello?"

"Claire, it's Gemma Johnstone. Your mother is working for me. Can you talk freely?"

"I'm alone."

"Good. I'll put your mother on."

The substance of the conversation was that Claire pack a bag of essentials for both herself and Louise and leave as quickly as possible. Louise began to give her daughter instructions on how to get to Buckingham Gardens by bus.

I held up my hand. "Tell her to take a cab. I'll pay."

With a terse injunction that Claire be careful, Louise hung up and went to speak to Mrs. Chisholm. I returned to the newspaper. Tim would no doubt want breakfast when he appeared, in exchange for which I would ask him to move the heavy dining table against the wall. Then I could lay out dishes and silver. Despite my lack of success with Brian, I felt in high spirits.

I was all set to while away a few minutes with the crossword puzzle, only to discover Brian had already done it—and in ball-point pen! I should have realized right then that he was untrustworthy. To do the crossword puzzle on the sly? And in ink? On just such shoals has many a relationship foundered.

She walks in beauty like the night
Of cloudless climes and starry skies.

So wrote Lord Byron, aristocrat, poet, and all-around good time. I have no idea for whom he wrote those lines, but he might well have penned them for Claire Laplante. The girl did walk in beauty, to such an astonishing degree that even I was brought up short. Confronted by a physical paragon one is drawn irresistibly towards the well-worn, not to say threadbare, encomiums: eyes like stars, teeth like pearls, hair like silk.

In the case of Louise's daughter, every well-worn simile rang
true. Tall, slender, with beautiful, high breasts, she moved with
the grace of a dancer. Above her mother's extraordinary cheekbones her widely set dark eyes, not unlike stars, were fringed with
lashes that threatened to trip her up. These were balanced by a
wide, beautifully shaped mouth whose teeth bore an uncanny
resemblance to: diamonds, emeralds, rubies, sapphires, pearls.
(Circle one.) More than flawless, her pale gold skin glowed with
the radiance that comes from being eighteen. Her long black
hair was combed straight back without a part, obliging her to
hold her head at a slight angle to keep the hair from falling across
her face. The look is currently fashionable with the young, and
in about fifteen years chiropractors will be treating women in
their thirties for disorders of the neck and upper spine.

Her natural shyness was magnified by the unusual situation of
having to sneak away from her own home like a political refugee.
She volunteered no information and answered direct questions
with a minimum of words. After paying for the cab I persuaded
her to let me make her some breakfast. I thought it would be a
good idea if Tim were to be downstairs before I took Claire up to
her room. As I made French toast I did not attempt to converse.
Louise had returned to her tasks, and with young people, as with
animals, it is wise to let them make the first move. Not to mention that it is difficult to hold a conversation with someone wearing
a Walkman. Although I had given Claire the newspaper, she
made not the slightest pretence of reading it. Most young people
are totally incurious about anything that does not directly touch
their lives.

I confess I rather looked forward to watching Tim's reaction
to Claire. How could a young and vigorous male in his early

twenties fail to react to this extraordinary beauty? And in his own king-sized way Tim was a handsome young man. The chemistry would be interesting to observe. I did not have long to wait. A heavy footstep announced that Tim was about to invade the kitchen. Swathed in a terrycloth robe, barefoot, uncombed, he came through the door. "Good morning, Miss Johnstone."

"Good morning, Tim. This is Claire Laplante. She and her mother will be staying with us for a couple of days. Claire, this is Tim Chisholm, Mrs. Chisholm's grandson."

"Hi, Claire."

By way of greeting she removed her earphones "Hi." Putting the earphones back in place, she turned her attention to the French toast which I set in front of her. Tim poured himself a cup of coffee and reached for the paper. When asked about breakfast he admitted to usually skipping it, but I encouraged him to try a cheese omelette, which I then began to prepare. Adrift in her world of sound, Claire ate her way through the French toast, while Tim read the op-ed page, uttering occasional snorts of disapproval. The two young people might have been brother and sister for all the attention they paid one another.

When I put the omelette and a stack of toast in front of Tim he gave me his high-voltage smile. "Thanks. Looks great."

"Would you like to go up to your room now, Claire?" I asked, just as Louise came into the kitchen. The girl did not reply; obviously she had not heard. Louise crossed to the table and yanked the earphones from her daughter's head.

"Miss Johnstone is speaking to you!"

The girl turned her beautiful blank face towards me.

"Would you like to go up to your room?"

"Yes, thank you."

"I'll take her upstairs," said Louise, picking up the suitcase Claire had brought. The two women left the kitchen.

"I hope you brought something to tie your hair back." Louise's voice carried from the stairs. "There's silver to be cleaned."

"Louise is having serious problems at home," I explained to Tim. "Your grandmother suggested she stay here for a couple of days, until she gets herself sorted out. Naturally she didn't want to leave her daughter alone with the man in question."

"Sounds reasonable," said Tim around a mouthful of toast.

"Claire is pretty, isn't she?" I asked.

"I suppose so. She is certainly exotic. But preserve me from women who wear Walkmans. I wonder if she takes it off when she's having sex."

"Tim, the girl is only eighteen!"

By way of reply he looked at me, then rolled his eyes upwards. I retreated to the stove in order to end an exchange I had no wish to pursue. I was also suppressing a giggle, beset as I was by the idea of two people having sex, each wearing a Walkman, each tuned to a different station. "Careful, darling, you'll dislodge my earphones." I suppose it beats, "Not tonight, dear, I just had my hair done." But only barely.

Before Tim went upstairs to shower and dress I asked him to move the massive dining room table. It could well have been an occasional table for all the effort it took. He also volunteered to drive me down the hill so I could visit my apartment and run a few errands for the party. We were running low on sherry, a popular pre-lunch drink with the elderly, and I needed to pick up eggs and bread for tomorrow's breakfast.

While he changed, I spread a cloth, resurrected from the top shelf in the linen closet, over the table and began to set out plates. By now Louise had chained her daughter to the kitchen sink where, earphones in her ears, rubber gloves to the elbows, she had been put to work cleaning silver. The girl was earning her keep, or, as Louise explained in an aside, "She might just as well polish silver as watch TV."

I was laying out damask napkins, yellowing from lack of use, when Tim came down the stairs, scrubbed and shining, his hair still damp from the shower. With Louise and Claire in the house I had no qualms about leaving Mrs. Chisholm. Tim and I climbed into the Jeep station wagon, the car he preferred to drive, and with a zoom backwards and a rakish C-curve, we took off merrily down the hill.

My idea had been to have Tim wait outside in the car, circling the block if necessary, while I dashed up to get my clothes for the party. As luck would have it, a parking space sat vacant right in front of the entrance, half an hour still paid for on the meter. Tim asked if he might come up; I saw no reason to refuse. After I had collected my dreary mail, bills and circulars, we rode the elevator to my floor.

The apartment looked tidy, although lightly coated in dust, my cleaning woman having been one of the first casualties of my new austerity. Tim, however, went straight to the paintings, peering closely at the surfaces, then taking a few steps backward to get perspective.

"Nice," he murmured, "very nice." Then he turned his attention to the drawing. "Matisse?"

"Yes."

"It's a good reproduction. But I suppose drawings are easier to reproduce than paintings."

"True enough." I did not think it necessary to point out that the drawing was original. At least he hadn't made the tired observation, as a cabinet minister once did, that his six-year-old daughter could have done better. My cleaning woman used to say the same thing, but when it comes to art, politicians and cleaning women have the same tastes.

I left Tim prowling around with, to my surprise, a more sophisticated curiosity than that shown by many a man twice his age. It took only minutes to put a few things into a bag, notably the dress I wanted to wear tomorrow, black jersey with a high, almost demure neckline in front, but plunging to a deep V in the back. Many men cannot help walking up behind me and placing their hand between my shoulder blades, making contact with my bare skin in a gesture at once more intimate yet less familiar than, say, patting my bottom. In the past it has been a useful little dress. With gunmetal pantyhose and black pumps, my hair down, I hoped that Brian would open his eyes and realize I did not go with the house, like wallpaper or the umbrella stand.

"All set?" I called out. Tim came out of the second bedroom, where I kept the television set.

"It's a great apartment!" he exclaimed with enthusiasm.

"I like the place, but it's a bit big, and expensive. I'm planning to move."

"What a shame! It has all the good features of a house, high ceilings, big windows, handsome mouldings. You should get yourself a roommate."

"Easier said than done, my lad."

"Here, let me take that." He reached for the suitcase. It was certainly pleasant to be around a young man with old-fashioned manners.

After stops at the market, liquor store, florist, all paid for from the roll of bills I planned to replenish on Monday morning when the bank opened, we drove back up the hill. At once I went to check on Mrs. Chisholm, who was reading in her armchair. We discussed what she would have for lunch, nothing too substantial as she would be eating dinner early. A chef's salad seemed the easiest solution.

I had bought frozen pizzas for lunch, one for Tim, one for the rest of us. Louise, Tim, Claire and I gathered around the kitchen table, an oddly assorted group. Tim, who had been taught to make the right moves, asked Claire what books she was reading at school. She thought for a minute, then reeled off some titles on her reading list, most of which she had not yet begun. She was working her way through a book about an old lady who ran away. Claire thought it boring. Tim let the matter drop.

Claire then volunteered a question, asking us about our astrological signs. I saw Tim's eyes glaze with boredom.

"I think I'm a Virgo," I volunteered gamely, "although the truth of the matter is that I was born over a sign, one that said 'Bass Ale.'"

Tim gave a small chuckle. Louise sat silent behind her dark glasses. I suspected she was in mild shock. Claire seemed lost without her earphones, the adolescent version of the security blanket. I was not at all convinced the girl was dumb, but I suspected she had never found herself in a situation where female intelligence was valued. Also beauty such as hers creates its own imperative. No current whatsoever flowed between her and Tim, at least not yet.

We finished our tea in silence, after which Louise returned to her duster and Pledge. Claire exchanged her Walkman for TV in the den and Tim disappeared upstairs to work on a term paper. I went in to settle Mrs. Chisholm for her nap. She insisted she was not sleepy, having done nothing all morning but read, but I was firm. She had to be in top fighting trim for tomorrow.

"But of course," she replied with a smile, as I pulled up the blanket to cover her.

While she slept I returned to the dining room. Claire had done a thorough job on the silver. It lay on trays, gleaming softly with the patina born of age and use. At either end of the table I laid out pyramids of forks. The knives I replaced in their slotted drawers as Fran was preparing food that did not require cutting.

It was pleasant to spelunk through the sideboard and breakfront. Setting the table for Mrs. Chisholm's party gave my frank curiosity the stamp of legitimacy. The house held everything necessary for a life of ease and grace. All it lacked was the will. In a silver bowl, newly polished, I arranged the flowers I had bought—white sweetheart roses, so as not to take up too much space on the table. Little by little the heavy and faintly forbidding room began to appear almost welcoming. Tomorrow, in disregard of daylight, I would turn on all the lights. Older people need more light in order to see, and lighted lamps are in themselves festive. To see a bulb burning during daylight hours means something a little out of the ordinary is going on.

There being nothing more to do in the dining room, I plugged in the kettle to make tea. Louise had chased her daughter out of the den so she could clean it. Claire had taken refuge in the kitchen, her earphones in place, her dark, luminous eyes fixed on nothing in particular, as she sat detached, calm, immobile. She seemed to be there, and at the same time absent. Had she levitated, or dissolved, or cloned herself, I don't think I would have been unduly surprised. What continued to astonish me

about the girl was her ineffable beauty, intimidating in its per-
fection. One could almost have wished for a slight flaw, a mole
on the cheek, a hook to the nose, one tooth out of alignment
with the rest, anything that would have made her appear less
ethereal. Perhaps etherial was not the right word. There was
something definitely tactile about Claire. Her golden skin invited touch; her long black hair would have seemed at home
spread across a pillow; her lithe stillness hinted at energy held in
check. The girl was an intensely sexual creature; I could well
understand Louise's concern about leaving her daughter alone
with an unstable man.

From the window I saw Brian's rented car pull into the driveway. I opened the side door and called out, "Tea's just made!"
With a wave he headed towards the kitchen door.

I decided I would simply introduce Claire to Brian without
footnotes. When I could get him alone I would explain how and
why she and her mother were staying over. In fact, explaining
the situation would give me a welcome opportunity to see him
alone. At the sight of Brian's tall figure coming through the door,
Claire removed her earphones, today's equivalent of standing
when an older person entered the room.

"Claire Laplante, this is Mr. Chisholm, Tim's father."

"How do you do, sir."

"Claire," he inclined his head. The three of us formed a triangle, so I was able to observe them both with minimum effort.

Perhaps I was lucky to be standing off to one side, as the look
Brian turned on Claire would have burned a hole right through
me like a laser beam. I know the look well. In the past I have
often seen that expression on a man's face, only he has been
looking at me. Eyes narrowed, lips parted, the man studies the

woman with such an intensity of desire that she is dehumanized, reduced to the status of object, transformed into a thing to be used.

If Claire registered his consuming glance, her face betrayed nothing. At that precise moment I realized I had been permanently relegated to the role of duenna or maid. What swept me with hopeless, irrational rage was not that Brian looked at Claire with pre-emptive desire, but that he would never unleash that same expression on me. I was frankly, furiously jealous; and as I have always been the one to provoke jealousy, not feel it, the sensation was disturbing and unpleasant.

Then a synapse kicked in. The neurons in my brain shot out impulses and it all came together. For most of my life I had made the arbitrary distinction between security and happiness, only to realize I had reached the age when security is happiness. Brian Chisholm meant security; security equals happiness. I did not love Brian, but I loved what he would have been able to offer: wealth and ease, position. And there he stood, so obviously besotted with the cleaning woman's adolescent daughter I was sorely tempted to hand him a strip of paper towel so he could wipe his chin.

Maybe the taste in my mouth was not that of ashes; I have never tasted ashes. But I recognized the bitter taste of defeat.

"I'll take some tea up to Mrs. Chisholm." I said to break the tension. "Please help yourselves."

When in the fullness of time I was able to remember this little episode with amusement, to run that meeting through the videocassette of memory without rancour, I could not help thinking of the operatic possibilities. The situation cried out for a trio in the bizarre theatrical tradition of characters singing their innermost feelings, seemingly oblivious to the others onstage.

Baritone:	I tremble. I burn. What is this sudden passion which consumes my soul?
Mezzo-soprano (Me):	I tremble. I burn. What is this sudden rage which consumes my spirit?
Lyric soprano:	I tremble. I palpitate. What is this sudden fear which troubles my heart?

As I carried tea up to Mrs. Chisholm, however, I was far from seeing the comic possibilities. What the hell! At least I wasn't going to cook dinner t. that sonofabitch.

"You look a little down in the mouth, my dear," said Mrs. Chisholm as I helped her out of bed. "Is anything wrong?"

"No," I lied. "I guess I'm just a bit preoccupied with the party tomorrow. Now, I'll give you a few minutes for your tea and a cigarette, then I'll help you dress for your evening on the town."

I returned to the kitchen to find Brian seated beside Claire and asking in an unctuous voice what television programs she liked to watch. I busied myself around the stove, filling the room with my presence and making more noise than necessary. I may have lost the fight, but goddammit, I wasn't going to be a good sport.

When Louise had finished the den, Claire took up her position once again in front of the TV. Brian followed, and I was treated to the sight of a man, nearly old enough to be Claire's grandfather and looking as though he'd stepped from the pages of a glossy annual report, pretending to be violently interested in rock videos. Maybe he couldn't see the screen; crotch fog blocks the view.

On the point of going up to help Mrs. Chisholm dress, I was caught short by the realization that I would be spending most of the evening with Louise and Claire. Louise I could handle, but I felt decidedly ambivalent towards Claire. I know she couldn't help being young and beautiful any more than a swan can change the shape of its neck. Claire had been no more than a catalyst, her mere presence triggering the reaction in Brian that I had failed to ignite. She could not possibly have understood my plan; her shooting me down in flames was devoid of malice. But that tired truth did not make me like her any better.

I telephoned Fran. "Sorry to drag you away from the Cuisinart, but would you like to have access to the kitchen here tonight? I have the evening off; the Chisholm clan is going out *en masse*. You have another pair of hands at your disposal, and it would be great to catch up."

"That might be a big help. Do you have refrigerator space for what I've already prepared?"

"There's a spare fridge in the basement."

"Terrific. I'll be over in about an hour."

In the interval I slapped together a meat loaf. I once read in a women's magazine—the kind that urges octogenarians to have a vigorous sex life—that meat loaf should be made with love. As love was in short supply at the moment I used ground steak. While I patted and shaped the mixture into the pan I half hoped Claire would turn out to be a vegetarian.

The principal protein for Sunday's lunch was to be steak-and-kidney pies. They sat baking in the oven. An exhausted Louise had gone to bed early, not surprising, as she had been hard at work since she arrived this morning and had probably not slept much after last night's hostilities. Claire had withdrawn to watch television in the den, while Fran and I were taking time out at the kitchen table with a bowl of ice and a bottle of vodka.

"So Mrs. Chisholm suggested—in fact she practically insisted—that Louise and her daughter come to stay."

"I had no idea," Fran dropped her voice, "that the girl was such a stunner. Is the grandson breathing hard down her neck?"

"Oddly enough he's not. But his father's been looking at her as though he were John Smith and she was Pocahontas."

"What's the father like?"

"Rich and single. What more do you need to know?"

Fran laughed. "That's not bad for a start. Is there anything else?"

"He's perfectly presentable: well-dressed, good looking—in that 'Men of distinction' way. All the warmth of an iguana." Warmed by the vodka I relaxed enough to laugh. "But just between these well-insured walls, I was quite prepared to make do. Then he took one look, just one, at our teenaged temptress and I put that little plan on hold."

Fran got up to check on her steak-and-kidney pies. "I guess he's one of those silly buggers who's trying to recapture his youth second hand. Sort of pathetic really. Everybody calls them dirty old men. Most of them aren't really dirty, just scared to death of growing old. And we all end up as a pile of bones, except for those of us who have had breast implants. Did you know those silicone transplants are not biodegradable?"

"No kidding, Fran. Pharaohs left pyramids while we leave plastic packets of gel. *Sic transit*. Let's have another little drop."

"One for the road."

"Do you know," I began to giggle, "he was sitting in the den with her watching rock videos?" We both started to laugh. "I'll bet you he never watches TV except for information: news, weather, and business reports. Never anything for entertainment, not even

Masterpiece Theatre. And he puts elastic bands around things, his cheque book, his engagement calendar. I peeked into his briefcase."

"If he's running around with an eighteen year old he'll have to put an elastic band around his you-know-what."

We smirked into our vodka.

"I'm seeing a guy now," said Fran. "He's so kind and considerate I still can't believe he's for real. He sends flowers; he remembers birthdays; he likes animals. He puts out sunflower seeds for birds and feeds the squirrels, mean little bastards that they are. And, my good woman, he goes to church. You heard me—church! It sure puts a crimp in Sunday morning sex." Fran took a swallow of her drink. "There is a downside, as you can well imagine. He likes sitcoms, especially those dealing with children. He likes jazz played on the violin. He likes to bowl. His idea of vacation is camping —sleeping bags, tent, mosquito netting, sterno stove, filtering coffee grounds through your teeth, the whole bit. I know, I know. I'm lucky at my age to have someone in the picture. But sooner or later I'm going to have to jump ship. I just can't handle all that goodness."

"A little goodness doesn't sound half bad to me. I seem to have spent a good deal of my life performing services for men that they wouldn't dare ask their wives to do. I've gone through gallons of Oil of Olay. I used to have a whole chest of drawers just for outfits, everything from strawberry pink baby dolls to a black leather cache-sexe. I've done interesting things with badger bristle shaving brushes, hot water and ice cubes, beads . . ."

"Beads? What the hell did you do with beads?"

I took another swallow of vodka. "Well," we both leaned forward, "I was going with this guy, and one night he turned up with a string of wooden beads, about the size of chick peas. He hemmed and hawed, but what he wanted was for me to introduce them into—into his anal orifice."

"Up his ass?"

"You've got it! Then we went about "it" in the usual way, right up until he was about to have his magic moment, when he hollered, "Pull out the beads!" This caused his sphincter to contract violently. I guess he enjoyed it; he sure made enough noise."

"What happened to him?"

"He wanted me to help him pull off a stunt, to make love in the conjugal bed. Many men entertain this fantasy, to screw the girlfriend under the family roof. It goes without saying the person really being screwed is the wife. I can still remember the room, powder blue flounces, ruffles, sort of a grown-up layette. Would you believe the wife burst in and caught us? Had I been set up? I covered myself demurely with the sheet while the couple ignored me totally and said a lot of boring and predictable things to one another. They reconciled—wouldn't you know—on condition that he stop seeing me. I had taken the precaution of being paid in advance for the caper, a rather pretty diamond bracelet. I never wear the thing, but it's nice to know it's there."

"I have to hand it to you, Gemma; you've done all the things most of us were too timid to try."

"Maybe. But you know something, Fran? I'm a bit winded. I'd like to slow down. I want a home and a garden and a garage where I can store the hose and the sprinkler. I'd like to go to the supermarket, and work on committees. The slow lane, for want of a better term, seems very attractive. But the way things look, it's back to work, the crisp white uniform and the white shoes that make my feet look like size tens. I haven't yet decided whether to stay on private cases or return to hospital work. I don't want to do either, but I have to pay the rent."

"The problem with men," Fran stirred the ice cubes in her glass with a finger, "one of the many problems with men, is that when it comes down to sex they become totally focussed on one thing. They never seem to remember that there is life after the Big-O, that you have to get out of bed and talk. Even if this Chisholm guy is turned on by teenagers he's still a fool to ignore all you have to offer. Even if he gets to first base with Claire, what then? What kind of relationship can they possibly have, even if the bumpity-bump is first class?" Fran finished her drink. "I suppose what I'm trying to say, Gemma, is that I think he's a fool for not slinging you across his white horse and galloping off into the sunset."

"I'd settle for a white limo. But thanks for the kind thought. I have to admit my vanity has taken a bruising, and you know as well as I do that vanity takes longer to heal than a broken leg."

Claire came into the kitchen. "Excuse me, but is there any juice?"

"In the refrigerator, top shelf," I replied.

By now the steak-and-kidney pies were done. Fran lifted them onto the stove to cool. "I guess that about does it for tonight. I'd like to come by early tomorrow, if you don't mind."

"Come whenever you like. I'll work around you to get breakfast, but after that I'll be out of your way."

We said goodnight and I watched Fran climb into her Audi. She took off down the street at a sporting clip, swerving sharply to avoid a taxi. I put the vodka back in the bar and emptied the remaining ice cubes into the sink.

The telephone rang. Had I been feeling charitable I would have answered the call upstairs so as not to interrupt Claire's program. Instead I walked into the den and told Claire in sign language to press the mute button. Misreading my message, she turned off the television and left the room.

As I lifted the receiver I thought of saying "Chisholm residence" in my most rounded tones, but I lost my nerve and offered the customary "Hello."

"Miss Johnstone, is everything under control?"

I recognized the voice as belonging to Christine Blake—the sound being as unmistakable as that of a police siren; but the same subversive impulse that made me interrupt Claire's program caused me to inquire, "Who is speaking, please?"

"It's Christine Blake!" she replied in the voice of a teacher barking out the right answer. "Is everything all right?"

"Perfectly, I am pleased to report. Where are you calling from, Mrs. Blake?"

"What does it matter? Put Mother on."

A week spent in the civilized company of Helen Chisholm had partially erased my memory of the daughter's rudeness. "I'd be glad to, but I can't. She has gone out for dinner." I knew I was dropping a depth charge, so I tried to sound nonchalant.

"She's what?"

"I repeat: she has gone out for dinner, with your brother and his son."

"But Mother never leaves the house unless it is absolutely imperative. How did she get downstairs? More important, how is she going to get back up?"

"She came down the usual way. If she has trouble climbing the stairs we will sit her in a straight backed chair, and Tim and Mr. Chisholm will carry her up." Prudence dictated I not let on that Helen had moved into her former bedroom.

"How could you have been so irresponsible as to let her go out of the house—and furthermore at night?"

"Mrs. Blake, I am not your mother's keeper. I am in her employ. She is in the company of her son and her grandson, both responsible adults. If you are going to level charges of irresponsibility, I suggest you direct them at your brother. It was his idea to take your mother out for dinner, not mine." The last was no less than the truth. Had my wishes prevailed, Helen Chisholm would never have left the house.

"Well then." Much as she longed to lay blame, even Christine had to concede I could not defy both mother and son. "Since everyone is out I don't see any point in drawing out this conversation."

"I'm managing very well, thank you," I replied in answer to the question she ought to have put. "When will you be returning to Montreal?"

She paused a moment before answering. "I'm not sure. I may stop over in New York for a couple of days *en route*."

"Very good. I shall sit tight until your return." A dial tone indicated she had hung up and that the conversation was over. I had to hand it to Christine Blake; her bad manners were incorruptible.

"All clear," I said as I pushed my way into the kitchen. Wordlessly, Claire rose and returned to the den and her interrupted program. Through the window I could see Brian's rented car turning into the driveway.

As he strode up the front walk, Tim grinned and waved. Helen Chisholm followed at a more sedate pace on Brian's arm.

"I'll take over from here," I said as they came into the front hall. "Are you ready to go up to your room, Mrs. Chisholm?" My reluctance to use her Christian name was compounded by Brian's presence.

"Yes, dear, I think I am."

Tucking her right arm securely under mine, I guided her up the stairs and into her armchair.

"Did you have a pleasant time?"

"Yes, indeed. We went to a delightful French restaurant, quite new to me; but then it's been years since I went out regularly. There was a menu, but the waiter stood beside our table and reeled off a long list of specialties, in French naturally. It was most confusing; we had to ask him to repeat most of it. Finally I decided on kidneys. Don't you think that when you go out you should eat something you don't ordinarily have at home?"

"Yes, I do." Mrs. Chisholm was still wound up with excitement over her outing, so I listened while she talked herself down.

"We were having such a pleasant time. I was drinking herbal tea because of the hour. I would gladly have stayed a bit longer at the restaurant, and so would Tim, but Brian seemed anxious to get back to the house. I guess he's had a long week."

"I guess." As I thought of Brian downstairs at this very minute trying to put the make on Claire, I wondered if perhaps the girl wouldn't have been better off with her mother's live-in.

"Would you like a glass of warm milk?"

"No indeed. Detestable drink. Save it for babies and pregnant mothers. And I'm much too old to worry about my calcium. I'm sure my bones are as porous as sponge."

As we talked, I helped Mrs. Chisholm out of the paisley silk and into a nightgown and robe. She was far too stimulated to sleep, so I sat in the chair facing hers.

"I'm glad we're having this quiet moment," she began, "as

there is something I would like to discuss." She paused to light a cigarette. "I have decided to move into Maple Grove Manor. Monday morning we will see about booking a place, after I have signed the deed revoking the power of attorney."

"What about the house?" I asked.

"I'll let Christine worry about that. She needs a roof over her head. She may well decide to sell. There will be only her and Arthur, and it's a lot of house for two people. I will furnish my own room and take a few mementoes. For the rest, I shall enjoy the enormous luxury of walking away from all these possessions. The whole lot will go to Christine and Brian sooner or later, so why not sooner?"

The old lady paused to inhale. "But all that is incidental to what I wish to discuss. Not to mince words, would you consider continuing in my employ? Wait a minute, my dear, and hear me out. You will not have to prepare meals and help me to dress. There is a staff at the residence to do all that. What I propose is to pay you a retainer. Then should I not feel up to going to the bank say, or taking clothes to the cleaners, you could run those errands for me. I will want to go out for lunch from time to time. You will come with me. And now that summer is just around the corner I would like to hire a car and take some outings into the country. Not for picnics. I detest picnics. There are excellent restaurants within two hours drive from the city."

Wordlessly I held out the ashtray, as the ash on her cigarette was beginning to curl.

"The point is, my dear, I do not wish to lose you once your two weeks are up. I know I am being selfish, but you have made such a difference to my life in only a few short days. I fully realize you have your own life to live and that it takes priority. That is why I wish to hire you on an *ad hoc* basis, so we can get together at mutually convenient times."

"You don't have to buy my time," I exclaimed. "I'd be happy to run your errands and go for delightful outings. Who wouldn't want to drive into the country for lunch?"

Mrs. Chisholm shook her head emphatically. "No, no, I insist on paying. That way I won't feel uncomfortable about having you spend time with an old lady, when I know you have dozens of other things to do. All I ask for the moment is that you consider my offer."

She paused to extinguish her cigarette. "Now I think I'll go to bed and read for a bit. You turn in too. Tomorrow will be a big day for both of us."

As I stood to help her to her feet and off with her robe, she embraced me. Surprised and touched, I returned the embrace.

"Please say yes to my proposal," she said as she eased herself into bed. "And now goodnight."

"Goodnight—Helen." At the door I paused. "Oh, by the way, while you were out your daughter called."

"Goodness me. Whatever for?"

"She was just checking up. She was very surprised to learn you had gone out for dinner."

"No doubt. What else did she manage to find out?"

"Very little. I said nothing about your having changed rooms, nor anything about the party. The subject of the cleaning woman never came up. She is under the impression that your son and your grandson practically kidnapped you—against my wishes."

Helen smiled. "Good. The less she knows, the better." She reached for her book. "Until tomorrow then."

On my way into the kitchen I paused to look into the den.

Seated side by side, Tim and Claire both leaned slightly forward towards the screen where a man, whose chiselled profile branded him a cop, was inching his way along a wall as he clutched a giant revolver with both hands. Off to one side Brian sat bolt upright, his posture suggesting boredom and impatience, even disapproval. The story on his press release would have been that he was sharing quality time with his son. The tabloid version might have suggested that he couldn't wait for this same son to bugger off so he could begin to put the make on the girl.

There was a ham-fisted irony in the present situation. At my suggestion, both father and son were spending the weekend under the family roof. By acting on a disinterested impulse I had brought the girl and her mother to temporary haven. Now we were all at cross-purposes, cancelling one another out like bubble gum and dentures. Claire had blocked my access to Brian, while Tim, simply by sitting in a chair and breathing the air, successfully prevented his father from trying to seduce a girl young enough to be his daughter.

The situation could have been funny. It should have been funny. But it wasn't. I longed for them all to go, to pick up the threads of their various lives and leave me alone with Helen Chisholm. She made me feel valuable, and at the moment I needed that feeling more than I cared to admit.

Eleven

*S*unday, a day I shall remember until I die or my memory goes, got off to an edgy start. I had slept fitfully, slipping in and out of a jittery wakefulness as insubstantial as the dreams that invaded my unconsciousness. I showered and dressed quickly, pulling on slacks I would eventually change for the little black dress, and went down to make breakfast. Brian, fully dressed, was already seated at the table. He managed to suggest, both by posture and a perfunctory nod of greeting, that I had been sleeping in and neglecting my duties.

The electric kettle could not have been easier to operate, leading one to suspect Brian Chisholm would prefer to go without and lay blame than to make the tea himself. While the machine hissed away, I boiled an egg and toasted two slices of bread. Brian retreated behind the paper, whacking the pages after he turned them as though they too were conspiring to annoy him.

"The yolk in this egg is hard, Miss Johnstone. Would you please cook me another."

"Right away, Mr. Chisholm. Sorry about that. I gave it a little extra time as it came out of the refrigerator cold."

Even as I spoke I realized he was a man who did not admit excuses. Now that I was no longer trying to win him over, I realized that life with Brian would not be easy. There might be a sound financial base and regular dividends, but the carrying charges would be high. You either got it right or you were in trouble. Obviously, things had not gone well with Claire last night. The most likely scenario was that Tim and Claire stayed up to watch *Saturday Night Live* before settling down to an early morning movie. A disgruntled Brian must have retreated to bed. His demeanour this morning suggested a frustrated lover. Well, screw him. I fished the egg from the boiling water when I knew the yolk would still be runny. So would the white. Before he had a chance to register disapproval I poured a cup of coffee and took it upstairs.

Mrs. Chisholm was awake but still in bed. She swung her legs over the edge. "Pass me my cigarettes, will you, dear?" she said as she pulled on her robe.

"How about a scrambled egg?"

"No thanks. I really don't feel like eating. And there will be heaps of food at noon."

As we weren't leaving the house today I let Mrs. Chisholm have her way. If she changed her mind I could always bring her a mid-morning snack. The doorbell summoned me back downstairs. True to her word, Fran had arrived early, the back of her car neatly stacked with baskets and cartons.

All traces of the broad had vanished as the businesswoman took over. From her hair, pulled sharply back and anchored at the nape, to her white blouse, black skirt, flat shoes, she was all crisp efficiency. Only the eyelashes, long enough to dust the furniture, hinted at the real Fran beneath the facade.

Brian had vacated the kitchen. I was not hungry. Mrs. Chisholm did not want breakfast. I suspected the young people would sleep away the morning. The only person unaccounted for was Louise.

I had just observed to Fran that Louise must be sleeping late, when she came into the kitchen. By now the bruise covering her eye was in full flower; not even dark glasses could hide what used to be called a shiner. I knew if I had a bruised eye like that, one, the man who gave it to me would be in traction and, two, I would not want to flaunt it in public.

"My God!" exclaimed Fran, getting right to the point, "that s.o.b. really socked you. First of all, is the eye okay? Do you think you should go to emergency?"

"No, it's all right. It looks a lot worse than it feels. The marks will fade in a couple of days."

"Louise," I said as I handed her coffee, "why don't you plan to work with Fran in the kitchen. I have a couple of friends coming who will be glad to help serve."

"Thanks," she said, reading my mind.

"Now girls if you'll excuse me," said Fran, "I don't need any help at the moment, but I do need to get myself organized."

Upon which she finished her coffee and began to unpack boxes. Leaving Louise to help if needed, I made a final tour of inspection. All was in readiness. The dining table lacked only food. The living room and den wore the faintly stagey look of rooms which await a party. Small, fragile ornaments had been hidden away so they would live to see another day. Stacks of paper coasters and cocktail napkins hinted at festivity to come. In addition to the regular furniture, chairs from the dining room had been grouped here and there, awaiting guests for whom standing could be difficult. The entire ground floor hummed with an expectant hush, an almost audible silence.

In that vibrant void, the sound of the front doorbell almost
made me jump. Wondering who it could be, I opened the door to
find Gerry and Luc on the doorstep.

"We've come in answer to your advertisement for a butler,"
Gerry began. "We don't do windows, but we sleep in and make
out."

"You're earlier than I expected," I said. "But come on in. Have
you had breakfast?"

"Never touch the stuff," replied Luc.

"You'll be glad we're here." Gerry pulled off his black leather
bomber. "If I got it right over the phone, this is going to be a
geriatric gathering. You will discover the golden oldies operate
within a fairly loose time frame. Which is to say that if you invited them for around noon they'll begin to arrive at eleven and
still be trickling in around two."

"Oh dear, I hope not. But I suppose you're right. Come and
have some coffee."

I led the way through the dining room and into the kitchen.
Fran looked up from the counter. "Ohmygod! Gerry!"

"Fran! You look like Joan Crawford in *Mildred Pierce*."

"I feel more like Marjorie Main in *Dead End*. What are you
doing here?"

"We were invited, by our gracious and lovely hostess."

"Fran, is there anybody you don't know?" I asked.

"I guess not."

"Gerry, Luc, I'd like you to meet Louise."

"Hi Louise." Gerry smiled his high voltage smile. "Have you
been pressed into service too?"

Louise smiled back by way of reply.

"Those cheekbones!" said Luc speaking for the first time. "To absolutely die."

"Gemma," said Gerry, "you must have some foundation somewhere in the house, and eyeshadow, and liner. We have to cover that bruise. There's a party coming up."

"Don't you think you should ask Louise?"

"Gemma, girl, nobody wants to walk around with a black eye. But—okay. Louise, do you want to stay as you are, or would you like to undergo a transformation that will have the whole world at your feet?"

Louise stifled a laugh. "That's a really tough choice."

"Go for it, Louise," said Fran. "We all look better with a little war paint. Oops! Sorry."

"And when you have finished making up Louise," I said, "would you mind preparing Mrs. Chisholm for the party? I know she'd love you to do her face. And she is the star of the production."

"But of course!"

When Gerry and Luc, working in tandem, had finished with Louise, we were all astonished with the result, the most surprised being Louise herself. One had to look closely to see the bruise, artfully concealed under makeup. Luc had combed and twisted her dark hair into a French braid, beginning at the crown right down the back of her head. Louise glowed. More restorative than even looking well was the attention. I would be willing to bet that Louise had not often been the centre of a man's attention except when he was either aroused or violent. But we all need stroking, physical and psychological. To be deprived of that kind of emotional contact is a form of starvation.

I was reminded once again that Gerry is what I consider a good man. He does not roll out of bed in the morning and jot down a list of worthy deeds to be accomplished. He does not consciously weigh his actions against some arbitrary standard of what others consider acceptable conduct. Instead he lays non-violent, non-sexual hands on women, and when he has finished they feel better about themselves.

And just as he had worked wonders on Louise, so did he perform a minor miracle with Mrs. Chisholm. I could have made her up myself, but having Gerry do her makeup for the party gave the event a feeling of occasion, even of ritual. We left her smoking and reading. At the last minute I would fasten her into the ivory brocade and bring her downstairs.

There is always a lull which precedes a party, a kind of void that beckons people to rush in and fill the vacuum with talk and laughter. Mrs. Chisholm waited only to be dressed. Brian Chisholm had retreated to his tower eyrie. Tim and Claire slept. In the kitchen Fran and Louise worked side by side, while Gerry and Luc passed the Sunday paper back and forth. I took advantage to ready myself for the afternoon's onslaught.

I had chosen my dress to help me make yards with Brian. That was before he met Claire. Still, I owed it to myself, to Mrs. Chisholm, to her guests, to look my very best, and it was with the ease born with years of practice that I enhanced my eyes and outlined my mouth. My hair, shampooed yesterday so as not to be too soft, fell almost to my shoulders. As I anchored it on the side with a broad gold clip set with a row of rather nice diamonds which, if challenged, I would say were paste, I wondered whether the time had come to have my hair cut short. For a woman who has always worn her hair long, to cut it short is a tacit acceptance of age. It was difficult enough to admit my age to myself. Did I want to confess to the world at large that it was time to shear?

I gave my hair a defiant shake. Like Scarlett O'Hara I would think about that tomorrow. Today I was wearing it down; further-more, I intended to have a good time. I was the one responsible for this party. It was to be Helen Chisholm's day; and the rest of us—Fran, Louise, Gerry, Luc, Tim—were here to see this day was a memorable success. I stepped into my high heels and finished off by liberally dabbing that good-old standby, *Fille d'Ève* onto temples, behind ears, throat, wrists, and behind my knees.

"Well, look at you!" exclaimed Fran as I made a perfectly timed entrance into the kitchen.

"Dress, where are you going with that woman?" laughed Gerry as he and Luc broke into applause.

"Name's Hayworth, Rita. 'I'm ready for my closeup, Mr. De Mille.' Actually I just pulled on the first thing that came out of the closet."

"Sure you did, honey," said Fran.

"Any sign of Tim?" I asked. "He is supposed to tend bar."

"Don't worry," said Gerry. "I can cover until he shows up."

As everything appeared to be under control, I went up to help Mrs. Chisholm dress. Time was sliding past, and soon the guests would begin to arrive. An energy field, larger than any indi-vidual, had been set in motion, and we had no choice but to let it carry us along.

I went into Mrs. Chisholm's room. "Would you like to dress now, or wait until the first guests have arrived?"

"I think I should be ready to greet them, don't you? I am the hostess after all."

"How are you feeling?"

"My stomach is a bit fluttery. But I intend to have a small gin when I go downstairs. Nothing settles the stomach like gin."

Showered and dressed, Tim stuck his head around the door.

"Morning, Gran, did you sleep well?"

"Yes, I did, thank you, dear."

"Something smells good in here." Then he caught sight of me. "Morning, Miss Johnstone."

"Good morning, Tim. Do you want breakfast?"

"No thanks. Claire and I had a sandwich late last night after the movie."

"Good. Some friends have already arrived. Go on down and introduce yourself."

As I laid the ivory brocade across the bed, Mrs. Chisholm butted her cigarette. With my help she stepped into the gown, which I pulled up onto her arms and fastened up the back.

"Are you going to wear any jewellery?" I asked.

"I hadn't really thought to. What would you suggest?"

"Maybe a pair of earrings."

"Let's have a look." Mrs. Chisholm crossed to the dresser and from the top drawer lifted a box in faded green calfskin with the Medici coat of arms embossed on the lid, the relic of a distant trip to Florence. Inside lay a jumble of rings, pins, clips, which looked as if they had come from an estate sale. Here was a woman wealthy enough to have bought my soul, and she didn't have one decent sized rock at hand. I chose a pair of pearl earrings, obviously fake, but the right colour for the gown. I also fished out three skinny gold bangles which she slid onto her left wrist.

"Will you wear a ring?"

"I think not. Now I am so arthritic I find rings on my fingers make me fidget." She picked around in the box and fished out an oblong ring made up of tiny garnets set in a cluster.

"Here, I'd like you to have this: a little memento of the day."

I have always thought of garnets as a kind of working-class

ruby. I would have scorned garnets from an admirer, but I found myself oddly touched by Mrs. Chisholm's gesture.

I slid the ring onto the fourth finger of my left hand. "Perfect, and just right for my dress. Thank you. Thank you very much. It's lovely."

She patted the hand wearing the ring. "Now I think I'll have one last cigarette before I go down. If anyone should arrive, please come and get me at once."

At the door I paused. "Do you suppose that in our contrasting black and white outfits we'll be taken for the Dolly Sisters?"

Mrs. Chisholm laughed. "My dear, you're not old enough to remember the Dolly Sisters. Let's hope they don't think we're Abbott and Costello."

A hum of voices came from the kitchen. "Welcome to the Downstairs part of *Upstairs Downstairs*," said Gerry as I walked in.

Tim sat at the table chewing on a hunk of bread spread with dip.

"I wasn't going to eat, Miss Johnstone, honest, but Fran insisted."

"I hate to see a grown man cry," she said as she slid a baking sheet of tiny pizzas into the oven.

"Miss Johnstone!" exclaimed Gerry. "Gimme a break! Do you supervise his homework and check his fingernails?"

Tim looked at me and we both started to laugh. "I guess it is pretty silly," I said. "I never stopped to think. My name is Gemma, Tim. Please use it."

We all jumped slightly at the sound of the doorbell.

"Ta-da!" sang Gerry. "Time to begin Operation Gemma. Places everyone! Damn the torpedoes—and full speed ahead!"

Almost to our relief the doorbell turned out to be a false alarm. Brian Chisholm had gone out for a run and forgotten to take his key. He stood on the doorstep in his expensively neutral jogging gear, sweating heavily, something I never imagined him doing, not even during sex. He acknowledged me with a nod and went upstairs to shower and change.

Brian probably ran regularly; otherwise he would not have carried a sweatsuit in his luggage. Today he must have run as though he really wanted to turn back the clock. I could only shake my head and hope he wouldn't be felled by a heart attack, at least not until after the party. I stood in the open door taking deep breaths. The air was fresh, not cold, and filled with a softness promising that April was only days away.

A car pulled up which I recognized as belonging to Edith Cross. She climbed out of the driver's seat, waved, and busied herself with unloading her mother and Mrs. Pitfield from the car and herding them up the path.

"Miss Brownstone," said Mrs. Pitfield, the hemline of her mauve crêpe hanging unevenly below her macintosh, "how good to see you again. I hope we aren't too late."

Edith caught my eye and rolled hers. "I would have thought we were invited for noon," she said, "but Mrs. Pitfield insisted the invitation was for eleven."

"So we split the difference," added Mrs. Potter.

"We're ready and raring to go," I said, standing aside to let them enter. Prompted by curiosity, Gerry and Luc had come to stand in the front hall. "Give these gentlemen your coats and go into the front room. I'll bring Mrs. Chisholm down. Just tell Gerry what you would like to drink."

"I think I might risk a sherry," announced Mrs. Potter.

"I never drink sangria," added Mrs. Pitfield, "too sweet. I think I'll have a gin."

"Our first guests have arrived," I announced as I entered Mrs. Chisholm's room. "Are you ready to go down?"

"As ready as I'll ever be." She extinguished her cigarette. "Do you suppose I can smoke during the party?"

"I don't see why not. It's your house, and you're the hostess. You make the rules."

Mrs. Chisholm smiled. "There you are. You see how much I need you around? Not that I want to pressure you into continuing to work for me. It's just that I won't take no for an answer."

"I'll bear that in mind." Laughing, I took her firmly by the arm and guided her down the stairs into the front room where she was met by a volley of greetings, voluble, predictable, formal as a gavotte: goodwill expressed in code. No sooner had I settled Mrs. Chisholm into the *bergère*, where she could hold court, than the doorbell rang. The party was under way.

Tim and I met in the hall. By way of bartender's uniform he wore a clean white shirt and a black bow tie. "Everything under control?" I asked, one of those pre-recorded questions that expects no reply.

He grinned, "Totally," then nodded his head toward the living room, humming with the sound of several simultaneous conversations. "Isn't it weird? Like something out of E.F. Benson or Barbara Pym."

"Take a good look," I suggested. "A couple of people in there are almost as old as the century. It's staggering to think of all they have lived through."

"Do you suppose they were aware of what was happening around them? Most of them sound as though they have spent the last fifty years on a desert island."

"You're probably right," I said. "They belong to a generation that managed to insulate itself from real experience, especially the women."

"I had no idea Gran had so many friends."

"Your grandmother is a very unusual woman, and evidently much loved. For not a few of those guests the effort involved in getting here was considerable, but they did it for her. I'm glad you're a part of this. You can remember her as she is today, bright, animated, surrounded by friends—not shut away upstairs like a crazed relative in a Gothic novel."

Luc crossed the hall carrying a platter of tiny brioches stuffed with chicken salad. "I'm rehearsing for my next movie," he announced. "I'm going to play a waitress, one of those tough, kind-hearted broads who knows she can make more money working the street as a hooker, but is clinging to her self-respect."

Tim let out a guffaw. "Does she have a handicapped, sorry—otherly-abled child back in her seven storey walkup?"

"But of course, darlink." Luc faked a Russian accent. "And don't forget the old blind mother who lost her eyesight making lace for the idle and unfeeling rich."

"I think it's been done," I said. "Tim, come and join the group."

"Thanks, but no thanks. We're having too good a time in the kitchen."

"I believe you," I said, not without a twinge of regret. How I would have liked to revert to 'below stairs,' setting out food, cracking jokes, trading gossip.

But duty beckoned. I went to rescue Brian, now showered, changed, infinitely presentable, who was being held hostage by Mrs. Potter, busily explaining the difference between a golf course and golf links. "Golf links are by the sea," she enunciated carefully, as though teaching him how to read.

"I've played at St. Andrew's," he said quietly.

"Mr. Chisholm," I said, "perhaps your mother might like another gin."

He gave me a look filled with gratitude and moved across the room. I eased Mrs. Potter into an adjoining conversation about proper storage of bulbs. A woman, whose malachite beads refused to collaborate with the neckline of her jersey print dress, tried to convince a man in gray pinstripe that an unheated garage was the best place for bulbs to spend the winter, didn't he think. His mouth was set in an uncompromising line suggesting he was prepared to answer no regardless of the question. Mrs. Potter, whose ignorance of the facts has never hindered her from holding an opinion, was shortly extolling the merits of a warm furnace room for keeping bulbs safe and snug.

I glanced around the room. Everyone appeared to be caught up in conversation. Most of the guests seemed to know one another, not surprising when one realizes English-speaking Westmount is a small town. All of the guests remembered Brian as a boy; he bore their gentle teasing with remote good humour. They were his people after all and they all appeared to be having a good time, within the somewhat narrow confines of their present capacity for enjoyment.

I was reminded of the elderly joke about the Boston matron who replied, on being asked where she bought her hats, "We don't buy our hats; we have our hats!" The same observation could well be made about the female clothes presently on display: two-piece dressmaker suits, one-piece outfits with matching jacket, afternoon frocks, cardigans draped over shirtwaists, and any number of sensible shoes. Mrs. Chisholm stood out in her gown, as did Poppy Pitfield in an eggplant satin bolero over the mauve crêpe chemise.

Edith Cross, wearing one of those frightfully good suits that can never be out of fashion because it was never in, crossed to inquire whether I needed any assistance with serving. I suspected her offer sprang in part from a genuine wish to help, coupled with a desire to escape from the company of people many years her senior. Edith is staunch; she does not flinch from bores. But she deserved a cigarette break, even if she didn't smoke.

"Let's go into the hall," I suggested, "where we can talk without shouting." The level of noise in the front room had risen considerably, a combination of sherry, scotch, and a guest list whose collective hearing had begun to fail.

"Do you think it's time to serve lunch?" I asked.

"Probably a good idea," replied Edith. "I've noticed a few of the men are using the party as an excuse to tie one on, no doubt in defiance of doctor's orders, and we don't want any accidents."

"You're right. I'll go and give Fran the green light."

The front door, left unlocked because of the party, flew open. Wearing her heliotrope travelling suit, Christine Blake strode into the front hall. She put down her makeup case with a clatter. "What on earth is going on?"

"Good afternoon, Christine," replied Edith. "Did you have a pleasant cruise?"

Cornered into civility, Mrs. Blake rose ungraciously to the challenge. "Edith, how are you? Miss Johnstone? It was horrid. I left the ship and flew home early. I repeat: what is going on?"

"Welcome back, Mrs. Blake." I moved to stand beside Edith, two against one. "We're just having a little lunch party for some of your mother's friends. Your brother is here, and your nephew. Please join us. Lunch will be served in a minute."

"I don't want any lunch," she replied rudely. "I'm going up to my room." Without further ado she headed for the staircase. The limousine driver carried bags into the front hall, touched his cap, and left, closing the door behind him.

At the foot of the staircase Christine paused. "Where's Mother?"

"In the front room," I replied.

Christine Blake paused for a moment, then strode across the hall into the front room. Totally ignoring the guests, she shouldered her way across to where her mother sat. Edith and I moved to stand in the doorway.

"Well, Mother, isn't this a surprise!" Something about the daughter's aggressive presence stilled conversation.

"Welcome back, Christine," said Mrs. Chisholm, "we're just having a little party. Do join us."

"I'm tired. I'm going up to my room. I'll speak to you when everyone has gone home."

"That won't be for a while," replied Mrs. Chisholm, refusing to be intimidated. "You're welcome to join us for lunch. I'd enjoy having you as a guest at my party." She looked directly at her daughter, silently willing the younger woman to pull herself together and be civil. I could have applauded.

"Mother, is that a cigarette?"

Mrs. Chisholm held the cigarette straight up and stared at it carefully. "It looks like a cigarette; it feels like a cigarette; it smells like a cigarette; and it certainly tastes like one. So, yes, it must be a cigarette."

"You know the house rule about smoking."

"Rules are suspended during a party, particularly one in my

own house. Here, would you like a Camel? I have plenty." Mrs. Chisholm smiled disarmingly at her daughter.

"You know I don't smoke," replied the latter. Short of snatching the cigarette from her mother's hand she had lost the skirmish.

Brian stepped forward. "Hello, Christine. Aren't you home early? We didn't expect you until next week."

"I left the cruise and flew to New York."

"Weren't you having a pleasant time?" he inquired, giving her the opportunity to explain her unexpected arrival.

"No," she replied without elaboration.

In his capacity as bartender Tim came into the living room. Catching sight of his aunt, he came over to give her a dutiful peck on the cheek. "Aunt Christine! Did you fly home just for the party?"

The harmless joke failed to amuse his aunt. "No, I did not. And I see you have been conscripted. I hope you're using a jigger to measure drinks."

"Yes, sir, ma'am!" Tim clicked his heels together and saluted sharply. A withering look loses its impact when the looker is several inches shorter than the lookee. By gazing straight ahead Tim managed to avoid eye contact.

Fortunately the gathering had picked up enough momentum so that Christine's arrival passed almost unnoticed, while the exchange with her mother and brother faded into the white noise of party chatter.

Abruptly, Christine strode across the hall into the dining room. I followed, anxious to exercise whatever damage control I could. Pausing only to scan the dining room like a security camera, she pushed her way through the swinging door to be brought up short by the unexpected scene of bustle and activity.

Fran looked up from the stove and, seeing my tight face over Christine's shoulder, broke open her high voltage smile. Only the most obdurate could resist that smile, but Christine didn't even flinch.

"Mrs. Sullivan, this is Mrs. Blake, Mrs. Chisholm's daughter. Gerry and Luc, who have volunteered to help out, and Louise I believe you know. Claire is Louise's daughter."

Christine acknowledged Fran with a slight nod and a barely audible "Mrs. Sullivan."

"How do you do, Mrs. Blake. I'd shake hands, but at the moment they're covered in flour." Fran continued to smile valiantly, a flashlight bouncing off a brick wall.

Christine grazed Gerry with her glance and brought it to rest on Luc. "Well, Luc, I didn't expect to find you here."

"If you'd like me to comb you out for the party I'd be glad to, just as soon as I've passed the crab brioches."

"That won't be necessary. What are you doing here, Louise?"

"Claire and I are helping Mrs. Sullivan."

The ranks closed. Christine found herself the focus of five pairs of eyes, not hostile, but not friendly either. Retreat was inevitable, but the intruder could not be flushed out of her own kitchen before firing off one last salvo. "See that you clean up the kitchen."

She pushed her way into the dining room. I followed in her wake. Crossing to where her mother sat, Christine towered over the older woman.

"I see you're using my plates for the party. What happens if a shaky hand drops one and it gets broken? That pattern has been discontinued."

"I could easily put out the other plates, if you wish," I suggested, conciliatory, anxious lest Christine disrupt the genial mood of the room.

But the daughter was no longer confronting a mother in braids, secluded in the tower room, easily intimidated. Christine was trying to face down Helen Chisholm, coiffed, made up, gowned, and with a couple of gins under her belt.

"Leave the plates, Gemma. If any of Christine's dishes should get broken I will smash the rest myself. Then she can start afresh with a more up-to-date pattern. Now, Christine, are you going to join us for lunch?"

"No—thank you. I'm tired. I'm going up to my room. Miss Johnstone . . . ?"

I followed her into the hall where she gave me a look of such distilled dislike that it almost singed the ends of my hair.

"Will you see that my bags are brought upstairs."

As she reached the landing I called out, "Would you like some lunch on a tray?"

She turned the corner without a reply. I waylaid Tim and asked him to carry the bags up to his aunt's bedroom.

"Should I wear armour?" he asked with a grin.

"I don't think that will be necessary." I wanted to add, "Be prepared to give your name, rank, and serial number," but decided to keep a discreet silence. My tact and diplomacy were beginning to give me heartburn; however, I still wanted the party to be a success.

As I crossed to the dining room I could hear laughter coming from the kitchen. How I wished I was part of it. I pushed open the door. "Fran, I think we could start slinging hash, if you're ready."

"Whenever you are," she said from the stove. "Give me five minutes to get the hot food onto the table, then turn them loose."

I returned to the front hall to find Brian standing with Edith. "Miss Johnstone, Mother sent me to look for you. She would like a word."

"Right away." I edged my way across the room to where Mrs. Chisholm sat. She indicated I was to lean close so she could speak into my ear.

"I'd like to go up to my room for a minute, if you'd be good enough."

"Aren't you feeling well?"

"Not very. It must be the excitement. If I could just lie down for ten minutes."

"Would you like some lunch? We were just about to serve."

"Not at the moment. And don't wait for me. Food will distract the others and make my disappearance less obvious."

I helped Mrs. Chisholm to her feet, and gripped her firmly under one arm.

"Just off to powder my nose," she fibbed as we edged our way towards the door. She leaned heavily against me, so much so I wondered about her managing the stairs. As if in answer to a silent wish, Tim came into the hall carrying a tray of glasses.

"Tim," I said low but urgently, "I need a hand. Would you take your grandmother's other arm and help her up to her room."

"Take the guests their drinks first," said Mrs. Chisholm, ever the hostess.

Tim lost no time, and in short order we were guiding Mrs. Chisholm, one stair at a time, up towards the landing. She was breathing heavily, each step an obvious effort. I don't think I could have managed without Tim.

On the landing we paused. "Would you like me to carry you the rest of the way, Gran? I could, easily."

"I have no doubt of that," Mrs. Chisholm rallied a faint smile, "but I can manage. Up we go."

One step at a time, Tim and I supporting most of her weight, Mrs. Chisholm reached the bedroom door.

"Thanks, Tim, I'll take it from here."

A few steps brought us to the bed, where Mrs. Chisholm half lay, half fell. As I lifted her feet and slid off her slippers, Mrs. Blake came to fill the doorway. "And whose idea was it that Mother move downstairs?"

"Mine," I replied without elaboration. "Your mother is not well. Will you please phone her doctor?"

"I know for a fact he is out of town. He was leaving only a few days after me."

"Then we had better dial 911. Your mother needs attention."

"Do you really think it's that serious?" demanded Mrs. Blake. "Maybe all she needs is a rest from all that excitement, or a nitroglycerine pill."

"I'm afraid nitroglycerine won't be much help," said her mother in a voice barely above a whisper. One look at Mrs. Chisholm, ashen and already semi-conscious, told me she required immediate assistance. I crossed to the telephone.

"I had hoped to arrive home to find the house running smoothly. Instead I find the place in an uproar and Mother having a seizure. What do you intend to do about the party?"

"To hell with the party! Your mother is ill." Angrily I punched 911 and requested an ambulance at once. I covered Mrs. Chisholm with an afghan and took her pulse, which fluttered ominously.

"Would you please ask your brother to come upstairs?"

"What do you need him for?"

Rage and panic burned behind my eyes. "Do as I say, you

stupid woman!"

A study in outraged dignity, Mrs. Blake stood tall. "May I remind you this is my house."

"No, it's not. It belongs to your mother. Now get out of my way!" I pushed past her and hurried downstairs. It was easy to spot Brian because of his height. "Mr. Chisholm, your mother is sick. I think she may be having a heart attack. I have telephoned for an ambulance." I tried to keep my voice calm, but anger broke through. "Could you please come upstairs and get your sister off my back."

He took the stairs two at a time. Christine Blake hovered uncertainly at the foot of the bed. By now it must have become obvious, even to her, that Mrs. Chisholm was seriously ill.

"Christine," he began quietly, "I know you must be tired from your trip. Why don't you go to your room. Miss Johnstone will see Mother into the ambulance and off to the hospital. Please, just go along."

Looking dazed, Christine Blake bowed to her brother's authority and retreated down the hall.

"Is there anything we can get her?" he asked.

"She wasn't taking any medication. All she has in her bathroom are the standard analgesics and nitroglycerine. But I fear this is more than just angina. I think it would be better to do nothing until a doctor sees her. Perhaps you should go and alert Tim. Ask him to watch out for the ambulance."

"And the guests?"

"Why not leave them be. As soon as the ambulance arrives they will know the truth, and the party will be over. You go on down. I'll stay here with your mother."

He nodded and left. Mrs. Chisholm opened her eyes.

"Gemma?"

"Here I am." I reached out and took her cold and flaccid hand.

"Was that Christine at the door just now?"

"Yes, it was. I guess she left the ship and flew home early."

"Oh dear. I suspect she had a row with Arthur. But even though she has come back, you won't leave me, will you, dear?"

"Of course I won't. I'll stay right here. I promise."

Her voice rallied slightly. "We still have so many things to do. I have to sign the deed revoking the power of attorney—and I have to engage a room at Maple Grove Manor. And you were going to take me to try on wigs . . ."

"As soon as you are back on your feet we will hire a car as usual and run all your errands. I wouldn't dream of letting you choose a wig by yourself. You'd lose your nerve at the last moment and pick something brown and safe instead of blond and flamboyant."

Mrs. Chisholm smiled faintly. "You know me too well. Now I think I'd like to sleep for a bit."

"I'll stay right here, Helen."

Those were the last words we spoke. Mrs. Chisholm closed her eyes. By the time the ambulance arrived she had slid into unconsciousness.

Twelve

*L*ater that afternoon I returned to the house. Waiting outside the emergency ward with only grim-faced people and a soft drink dispenser for company does little to help the patient. Brian, who followed the ambulance in his rented car, had gone out to stretch his legs. When he returned, the news was the same, meaning no news at all. He urged me to return to Buckingham Gardens, report to Christine, and suggest maybe she come down to relieve him for a while.

Aside from my physical presence, I could not have been very good company. All during that long vigil outside Emergency I asked myself repeatedly whether I had been negligent, ignoring symptoms of the incipient stroke. I was a nurse after all. Although I had not worked for a while, I still possessed a degree of medical sophistication far beyond that of the ordinary person. Ought I to have suspected Helen Chisholm was ill? I revisited the past twenty-four hours, like someone playing and replaying a videotape, searching for missed clues. Yet aside from her natural excitement, her heightened awareness, I could remember nothing that should have made me suspicious. It had, after all, been her legs and not her heart that caused her to fear stairs. Had I not been so preoccupied with my own concerns—my failed attempt to seduce

Brian, my preparations for the party—might I have saved her this terrifying trip to Emergency? The question was rhetorical at this point, but that realization did not help.

Had I been irresponsible in allowing her to smoke? Very possibly, but did not the evident enjoyment she obtained from cigarettes more than compensate for the risk? A lifetime of heavy smoking must have done far more damage than the few packs she had inhaled during the past week. She was an old lady; her life of semi-incarceration in the tower room could only be described as sedentary. All these factors added up to high cardiac risk, not to mention the sudden intense stress of having her disagreeable daughter burst in unexpectedly. Yet the interest and enthusiasm she had shown for our outings and projects had convinced me her principal complaint to have been sheer boredom. I had no way of telling, and an indulgent wallow in self-recrimination was not about to help the patient.

At Brian's insistence I left the hospital. There was absolutely nothing I could do, but I couldn't avoid the irrational feeling that my very presence was sending out positive vibrations. Whenever I sit in the passenger seat of a car I am reluctant to take my eyes off the road, regardless of who is driving, believing that a moment's inattention on my part could spell disaster. By the same token I secretly believed that were I to leave the precincts of the hospital, Helen's chances of survival would be diminished. The strength of an idea often bears little relation to its quotient of common sense.

I took a taxi from the line outside the hospital, which I paid for with a twenty dollar bill Brian had given me, as in the confusion of leaving the house I had forgotten to bring my bag. That meant I did not have my key. I had put both doors on the latch for the party, but in the interval they had been locked. Reluctant to ring and bring Christine downstairs—she could still be asleep—I remembered the key hidden in the garage, the one Tim had told me about.

I had left a house alive with people; I entered what felt like a crypt. All traces of the party had been erased. Even the dining room table stood in its rightful place, surrounded by the appropriate chairs. The kitchen looked as though it had not been used in a week. Only an orange light on the control panel of the dishwasher gave a hint of recent activity. The silence was dense, heavy, palpable.

A quick glance into the living room and den told me the mopping up process had been absolute. Not even a stray toothpick remained to suggest only hours ago people had laughed and conversed in these rooms. I went quickly up the stairs. The door to Helen's room stood shut. Cautiously I opened it and looked gingerly inside. The bedspread still showed creases where Helen had lain while we waited anxiously for the ambulance. Automatically I leaned over to give it a tug, smoothing out the wrinkles and patting the pillows back into shape. As I straightened up I realized I was no longer alone.

"Mrs. Blake, I was just about to look for you. I'm glad you're not asleep."

"Asleep!" she repeated as though it were a four letter word. "I had to clean up the mess after that slatternly caterer left."

Having watched Fran work, I know she wipes up every crumb, but now was not the time to point that out. "Your brother could use a little moral support. He is reluctant to leave the hospital until your mother's condition has stabilized."

"I was just on my way down." Christine Blake was dressed to

go out, in an olive green suit with burnt sienna blouse. The suit was beautifully cut, but olive green makes blonds look sallow.

"Now that you have returned, Mrs. Blake, what would you like me to do? Your mother will probably need nursing care for a while, and I am a registered nurse. Furthermore, I would like to remain on the case."

"What I would like you to do, Miss Johnstone, is to pack your bags and leave my house."

"I understand you would prefer to be alone at the moment. I am just about to collect my things and go. However, before I find myself another job, which I will have to do, I would like to know if you want me to nurse your mother . . ."

"If I find you going near my mother I will have you arrested. I leave you in charge for one week, not even that long—and I return to find the house in chaos and Mother having a heart attack from too much excitement and too many cigarettes."

We faced one another across the bed, like two prizefighters exchanging insults from their respective corners.

"Excuse me, Mrs. Blake, but the house was not "in chaos," as you put it. We were merely having a lunch party, for a few of your mother's friends, whom she had not seen for quite a while. And to say her attack was caused by excitement is hardly a sound medical diagnosis. True, I did not keep her incarcerated in the tower room, like the mad Mrs. Rochester, and I did not deny her cigarettes, but that is because I realized she was dying of boredom."

"She was not dying—as you so quaintly put it—but she may be now, thanks to you." Christine Blake assumed the smug expression I am sure she wore after sinking a fourteen foot putt.

In spite of good intentions my temper was beginning to fray.

I fought to keep it in check.

"Mrs. Blake, you waltzed out of the house for two weeks, leaving me with no instructions, no emergency phone numbers, one hundred dollars mad money, and the responsibility for both your mother and this large house. I did what I thought best. If my program does not meet with your approval, that is unfortunate. I will not say I'm sorry because I'm not. I would suggest, however, that you watch your irresponsible accusations. I set out to give your mother a pleasant time, not to do her in—as you insinuate."

"On whose authority did you move her downstairs and provide her with cigarettes? On whose authority did you go into my bank and withdraw funds from my account? And who gave you permission to turn the house upside down, and furthermore, to hire a caterer. You were being paid to do the cooking."

"The answer to all those questions is your mother. She wanted to move downstairs. She bought her own cigarettes. She signed the withdrawal slip; I did not forge your signature, believe it or not. And she authorized me to engage a caterer. It is her house after all."

"Only in theory. I have her power of attorney."

"Not any more, you don't. As soon as Mrs. Chisholm is well enough she will sign the document revoking your power of attorney. It has already been drawn up."

That slowed her down. Perhaps I had been indiscreet in mentioning the as yet unsigned revocation. But I really wanted to stick it to this overbearing bitch.

Unfortunately she rallied. "If the document has not yet been signed then the power of attorney is still valid. That means I still remain in charge. I want you out of here—and now!"

I switched tactics. "Mrs. Blake, why did you leave the cruise early and fly home?"

Coming out of left field, the question caught her off guard. She tensed as if expecting a blow. "That is no concern of yours."

I pressed my advantage. "Was it because your husband, who comes on to anything female that is standing still, got involved with another woman?"

I thought it was only in Victorian novels that women changed colour, but angry red blotches erupted across Christine's face.

"How dare you!" She stalked to the door, then turned. "I am going down to the hospital. If you're not out of here by the time I get back I shall call the police."

"That won't be necessary," I replied. Having rousted the enemy I could afford to be conciliatory. "I will pack and leave at once. Mrs. Blake?" At the sound of her name she turned. "Let me give you a word of advice, woman to woman. Unload that husband of yours. He's a bimbo." I smiled my sweetest smile.

The telephone on the night table rang. I picked up the receiver. "Hello?"

"Miss Johnstone, is my sister there?"

"Yes, she is. Just a minute. It's for you," I said to Christine Blake, still standing in the doorway. "It's Mr. Chisholm." She crossed the room to wrench the receiver from my hand.

"Brian?"

I could hear the sound of a voice on the other end but was unable to make out the words.

"I see," said Mrs. Blake. "I'll go downstairs and wait for him." She replaced the receiver in the cradle. "Mother just died," she said without emphasis. "Tim is coming to pick me up." As she moved past me to get to the door she paused and turned. Then, as casually as if she were reaching up to tidy her hair, she slapped me.

The woman was strong, but having been in my share of dust-ups as a teenager, I could see the blow coming and rolled with it, backwards onto the bed. Even so, she still managed to connect with enough force to make my cheek burn. Pain turned me from merely angry into furious. I rolled off the far side of the bed, kicking off my shoes in the process: you need purchase if you are going to sock someone. Then I gave her the old one-two, left to the abdomen, right to the jaw. Mother always used to say a lady hits with an open hand, but I wasn't feeling very ladylike at the moment.

That lean, tough body took the blows with hardly a tremor. I ducked just in time to avoid being crowned with *Webster's Collegiate Dictionary*, which Mrs. Chisholm kept on the vanity table to consult for her crossword puzzles. The book sailed from Christine's hand, landing harmlessly in the fireplace. When she reached for Boswell's *Life of Johnson*, a weighty tome with a murderous spine, I took refuge behind an occasional chair. Holding it by the front of the seat and a bar across the back, I threatened her with four brass-tipped legs while she brandished the lethal *Life*.

"There was a time when you could have blamed your behaviour on PMS," I suggested, "but not any more."

At this point Tim walked into the bedroom.

For a moment we formed a *tableau vivant*, Christine holding Boswell as though it were a football, I in a half crouch wielding the chair, Tim immobilized with astonishment at the door. The freeze frame dissolved.

Casually I lowered the chair. Just as casually, Christine put the book onto the vanity. Only *Webster's Collegiate*, lying on the hearth like a wounded seagull, suggested anything amiss.

"Aunt Christine, are you ready to leave?"

"Yes." Moving to sit at the vanity she took a second to smooth her hair only slightly mussed in the melee. "Let's go," she said as she stood. As she passed me en route to pick up the bag she had left on the dresser, she paused. Fully believing that Tim's presence had defused the situation I had dropped my guard. This time the slap caught me with full force, snapping my head sideways.

"Aunt Christine!" exclaimed Tim, his voice hoarse with shock.

Fortunately for me she paused, just long enough to give me that look, the one she wore when she sank her approach onto the green. As she turned to move away I was ready. Hooking my stockinged foot around her left ankle, I kicked sideways. Down she tumbled, with a crash and a cry. That fall must have hurt, almost as much as my inflamed cheek.

This must have been a first for Tim, seeing two women going at one another, the way they used to in the movies. Saucer-eyed and speechless, he helped his aunt to her feet and led her away, limping. I stood in the middle of the room, breathing heavily, until I heard the front door close behind them. I was alone in the house.

Once again I smoothed the coverlet, rumpled by my fall. I picked up the damaged dictionary and put it on top of Boswell, neatly lined up with the edge of the vanity. After casting one final look around the room where Helen and I had spent so many pleasant hours, I went out and shut the door.

I took only minutes to fold my clothes into suitcases—the man's shirt, slacks, green silk dress, Peter Pan blouse, and finally my neo-Grecian *peignoir*. Briefly I thought of changing out of my black jersey, which felt crumpled and stale, but so eager was I to leave that depressing house that I almost threw my toothbrush and comb into the case.

Downstairs in the front hall I assembled my small suitcases, makeup bag, handbag, and coat. From my purse I took the small account book I had bought to keep track of expenditures. Inside the cover I tucked the cash remaining from the one withdrawal. With every last dime accounted for, I left the account book on the hall table.

After telephoning for a taxi I made two trips to ferry my things to the edge of the sidewalk. Pulling the front door shut, I used my key to turn the deadbolt with a faint but final click. I pushed my key through the letter slide; it tinkled onto the tile floor.

For what seemed like hours I waited beside my bags for the taxi to arrive. By now the adrenalin high resulting from my fight with Christine had drained away, leaving me so empty and exhausted I was tempted to sit on the edge of the sidewalk. Not once did I look back at the house, not even when we drove away. Instead I twisted the garnet ring on my finger, the one Helen had given me just before the party. As we rounded the corner I was swept with the aching realization that Helen Chisholm was dead. In less than a week I had found and lost one of the best friends I ever had. Turning my face away from the rear window, I wept.

Once back in my apartment I peeled off the black jersey and took a long, hot shower. I shampooed my hair twice. Standing under the warm, restorative flow, I knew I was wasting water, but I didn't care. After drying myself and wrapping my wet hair in a towel, I pulled on a robe, terrycloth and non-Grecian, before settling down with the telephone.

I called Fran to tell her about Mrs. Chisholm and to learn

what had happened while I was at the hospital. Stunned by the turn of events, Fran had to pause a moment before she could speak. Ordinarily she throws herself into telling a story, not altering the facts but giving them an energetic spin. The news of Helen Chisholm's death slowed her almost to a stop, and she related what had happened without elaboration.

Nothing kills a party faster than watching the hostess being carried out on a stretcher. As soon as the ambulance had driven away, most of the guests followed suit. Lifts were offered, taxis ordered, and the two ladies who had arrived in their own limousines each drove away with a full car. Only Poppy Pitfield refused to leave, announcing in her shortwave voice that dismay over her friend did not obviate the fact that she was hungry. Her resolute determination to eat meant that both Edith Cross and her mother would have been obliged to stay. Edith tactfully suggested buying them all lunch at a downtown restaurant, and the reluctant Poppy was led away.

As there remained mountains of untouched food, Fran had insisted the support staff—Louise, Claire, Gerry, Luc, and Tim—help themselves. They were just digging in when Mrs. Blake came downstairs and told them to clean up and clear out.

A woman not easily intimidated, Fran asked to whom she should send the bill for catering the lunch. She explained she had been given two hundred dollars on account, but she had receipts for what she had spent. If Mrs. Blake wanted to pay her cash she wouldn't charge sales tax.

"And who gave you the two hundred dollars?" Christine had demanded.

"Miss Johnstone," Fran had replied.

"And where, may I ask, did she get the money?"

"How should I know? Surely your mother must have an account."

"Well, well, the mice have been busy," Christine had observed. Abruptly she stalked from the dining room and retreated upstairs to barricade herself behind closed doors.

"Where did Louise and Claire go?" I asked Fran.

"They're here with me, until they find a place of their own. It's a bit cramped, but we'll manage."

"In the meantime, Mrs. Blake said nothing about paying you?"

"Not a word. I know it sounds unfeeling to discuss money, with a funeral in the offing, but I'm quite heavily out of pocket."

"You don't have to explain, Fran. I haven't been given a penny of salary either. And the Blake woman hates my guts, so she isn't going to cough up a cent without a struggle. If worst comes to worst we can take her to small claims court. The problem is that she can afford to hire the best lawyers. Keep your receipts though. Be sure you can account for everything you have spent. I have an idea I want to pursue first. Leave it with me."

We rang off. I felt angry and impotent. There was Fran, in debt for a party I had engineered, and quite probably going to be bilked. At the same time she was falling over Louise and Claire in her small apartment, while Buckingham Gardens stood empty.

Cradling the phone in my lap, I took out the telephone book and checked the listings for Chisholm. There was a number for one T. Chisholm on a street in the student ghetto. It had to be Tim's number. I was on the point of dialling, when the phone began to ring, causing me to jump from surprise.

"Gemma," said a man's voice, "it's Neil."

"Neil! Of all people! Where are you?"

"New York. I just got in from Bermuda. But I'm flying up to

Montreal on business tomorrow morning. How about tomorrow
night?"

"Sorry, Neil, I can't. I'm tied up."

The fib came out so easily that I surprised myself. No engagement of any kind prevented me from seeing Neil, having a good
time, and walking away with cash in my handbag.

Neil Buckley had moved to Bermuda because of the island's
lenient tax laws; however, business and boredom brought him
north frequently. I had been seeing him on and off for years.
Aside from a tiresome habit of talking about my Bermuda triangle, he was fun to be with. More important, he was generous
to a fault—never a fault in my books—but with high income and
low taxes he could afford to be.

"Can't you get out of it? I only have the one night to spend
in Montreal. I'd be glad to up the ante."

"I really am sorry, Neil, but—believe it or not—I have a
regular job. I'm working as companion to an old lady, and she
can't be left alone at night."

Even now I find it difficult to explain the lie. Nothing
whatsoever kept me from seeing Neil except a kind of reluctance
I found difficult to explain. My sense of my own worth had never
sprung from refusing men. On the contrary, being available has
stroked my ego and bolstered my income. Yet I found myself
suddenly unwilling to be there for a man, even one I liked, who
understood all it took was a telephone call and a handful of
banknotes to fuck me as he pleased. Whether or not I saw Neil
would change nothing, other than giving me some badly needed
cash. But that small, insistent voice could not be ignored.

"That's nothing but a form of glorified babysitting," he continued. "Find someone to fill in for you. Companions are a dime

a dozen. High-powered redheads aren't. How about I double what I ordinarily drop into the vase?"

The offer knocked me speechless. We were talking major money, enough to make me solvent. And playing rollaround with Neil was not unpleasant. He was bright and amusing; he had beautiful skin, golden smooth from the Bermuda sun. His pot belly never got in the way when we made love. I never had to fake it with Neil.

"Well, kiddo, how about it?"

I rallied my faltering reserve. "I can't, Neil. I've given my word."

"You know what the Bard says, Gemma: 'He's mad that trusts in the tameness of a wolf, a horse's health, a boy's love, or a whore's oath.'"

"You know something, Neil? The Bard said far too much, about everything. I have a responsibility to fulfill. Surely you can respect that."

"'The lady doth protest too much, methinks.' You know perfectly well you're going to say yes, so why don't you just set a time."

Maybe it was all that damn Shakespeare, perhaps it was his smug male certainty, possibly it was the overwhelming temptation of all that easy money warring with my own sense of—what, decorum perhaps? But suddenly I was angry. "I don't care what your bloody bard says, Neil. I have agreed to do a job, and I am going to meet my commitment, whore's oath or not!"

"So I won't see you tomorrow night?"

"No."

"Well then. Goodbye, Gemma. Good luck."

As I replaced the receiver I was swept with regret. I had just set fire to my last bridge, and the acrid smoke made my eyes water. To think I had turned down a good and profitable time for nothing more than a vague feeling that Helen Chisholm would not have approved. But Helen was dead. I couldn't even be sure she would have disapproved. She understood the pleasure principle and the obligation to make ends meet, or she had. But the idea of Helen laid out in an undertaker's parlour would have made it impossible for me to be the "high-powered redhead" of Neil's imagination. I had chosen to live in my own reality, not in another man's fantasy.

I knew Neil would never call me again. For him I was a commodity, and when a certain commodity is not available, a businessman will look elsewhere. For something as intangible as a little belated self-respect I had bartered away the last link to my former life of good times and no questions asked. Tomorrow I would make an appointment with Gerry to have my hair cut. I would also buy myself a couple of white uniforms. The cold consolation of knowing I had perhaps made the better choice could not erase the nagging, uncomfortable feeling that I had been a fool.

When I finally managed to reach Tim, who had taken his father out to dinner, I learned the funeral was to be strictly private. The arrangements had occasioned a major row between brother and sister. Brian understood I would have wanted to attend, as would Poppy Pitfield and many of those present at the interrupted lunch party. So anxious was Christine Blake that I not attend the funeral, she refused to be budged. She held me personally responsible for her mother's death. And my having punched her out and tripped her up had only added fuel to a burning dislike. Helen Chisholm was to be buried from Buckingham Gardens with only the immediate family present.

"Did that include Arthur Morris, the absent husband?" Brian had wanted to know.

Then, as Tim put it, the faeces hit the fan. Aunt Christine had taken off. Arthur Morris had involved himself in such a scandalous shipboard romance that she had left the cruise in Puerto Rico and flown home. It seems he didn't even have the taste to get involved with another passenger, but had pursued one of the cocktail waitresses. He then coaxed her into the stateroom where Christine, returning early from an onshore shopping trip, had discovered them. Monday morning she was seeing her lawyer about a divorce.

Brian had inquired whether Christine and Arthur had opted out of Bill 146.

"Bill 146?" Christine had demanded. "Whatever do you mean?"

Brian explained in broad outline that those couples married prior to July 1989 had been obliged to sign an agreement opting out of the family patrimony law no later than December 31, 1990. Otherwise, in case of divorce or death, certain properties acquired during the marriage had to be split equally. Instead of ending up severed from his wife's considerable wealth, Arthur Morris could walk away from the marriage with a handsome settlement. Christine had done nothing about the legislation, meaning she had to submit to the provisions of Bill 146 and split assets with her estranged husband.

Baffled and furious, Christine had cast about for scapegoats, finally falling back on the ancient custom of slaughtering the messenger bearing bad news. She rounded on her brother, berating him for a variety of grievances, some dating back to their childhood. Finally, she concluded by saying that if necessary she would hire security guards to make sure no one but immediate family attended the funeral.

Brian waited until she had finished, bowed, went upstairs to pack, and asked Tim to drive him to the Four Seasons Hotel in the rented car.

"So that's the score at the moment, Gemma," concluded Tim. "Father and Aunt Christine aren't speaking. Her marital situation is decidedly murky, all of which may help to explain her uneven disposition. And the funeral is to be private. Sorry about that; I know you would have wanted to be there. The scoreboard reads: Lions five, Christians zero."

In spite of myself, I laughed. "We really don't need to watch the ABC Movie of the Week. We're playing in it. Thanks for filling me in. Perhaps you could let me know where your grandmother has been buried. I'll go and pay my respects at the cemetery."

"I'll take you there myself."

"I don't want to put you out."

"You won't. I'd be happy to." We said goodnight.

There are times in a woman's life when a glass of gin is the only solution. I have always been a moderate drinker, but I kept my bar well stocked for my gentlemen callers. I broke the seal on a bottle of gin and poured a generous shot over ice cubes in a tumbler. The first swallow hit my stomach with a tiny explosion, leaving me breathless, followed by little aftershocks of warmth shooting through my arms and legs. Fortified by the albeit temporary courage, I telephoned the Four Seasons Hotel and asked to be connected with Mr. Brian Chisholm's room. After a few rings his voice came onto the line.

"Mr. Chisholm, it's Gemma Johnstone. I hope I'm not calling at an inconvenient time."

"Not at all, Miss Johnstone. What can I do for you?"

"I have something I would like to discuss with you, *à propos* of your mother. I would offer sympathy, but somehow it seems so inadequate. I feel too badly about her death to offer platitudes."

"I quite understand. Now, tomorrow I have a breakfast meeting, then an appointment. But I will return to the hotel before lunch. Could you come to my suite, say, around eleven-thirty?"

"That would be just fine. I will be there. Thank you. Oh, and Mr. Chisholm . . ."

"Yes, Miss Johnstone?"

"Oh, nothing I guess. I was going to say something about Mrs. Chisholm, but over the telephone it wouldn't have sounded the way I would have wanted it to sound."

"I know what you mean. But I appreciate the thought. Until tomorrow then."

With the telephone on my lap I finished the gin, somewhat diluted by melted ice. There were more calls I ought to make, to Gerry, to Edith Cross; but talking on the telephone takes energy. You have only your voice to carry the message, totally divorced from gesture, body language, context. Ordinarily I don't mind, but in spite of the gin I found my energy level very low. When the telephone on the floor beside my chair began to ring, it was almost with relief I picked up the receiver. Whoever it was had taken the initiative; all I had to do was say hello.

"Gemma, it's Gerry. I wanted to find out how Mrs. Chisholm is doing. Is she up to having visitors?"

"She died this afternoon while still in intensive care. She never regained consciousness."

There was a pause. "I see. I'm so sorry. Are you going to the funeral?"

"I can't. The daughter threw a fit and insisted the service be private." Briefly I filled in the details of my conversation with Tim.

"Bummer," said Gerry. "She sounds like ten miles of bad road."

"I won't be sending her a Christmas card, you may be sure."

"Can I come over? I won't stay long."

"Sure, why not. Is Luc with you?"

"No, he's visiting his father. Every Sunday night, rain or shine, he spends with the old man."

"Good for him. I must warn you I'm in a terrycloth robe and I'm not going to change."

"I'm wearing a tux, but try not to notice. See you."

I decided against phoning Edith Cross, at least until tomorrow. Bad news travels faster than the speed of light and by now she probably knew. Even if she hadn't heard about Helen's death, there was no funeral to attend. A great many things waited to be dealt with tomorrow, "The first day of the rest of my life," as a bumper sticker would have it. I postponed that threatening tomorrow by pouring myself another shot of gin.

"Don't move! I want to remember you just the way you are!" Gerry held his hands as if framing a shot. I opened the door wide enough to let him enter.

"Would you like a drink? I'm already into the gin."

"Sounds good. Gin was Mother's ruin, but she died a happy wreck."

"I want you to understand I'm not drinking it because I like it. I just want something to put into the blue recycling bin."

"I can't think of a better reason."

I poured him a drink and we sat. "What do you generally do on Sunday nights," I asked, "with Luc tied up?"

"Not much of anything. Luc's father doesn't like me. I don't know whether he suspects the truth, but I stay away. Time was when I used to go to the bars. It was pleasant on Sunday, more low key, less frantic and desperate than Saturday night. I'd do a little window shopping. Sometimes I'd even try on the merchandise. But not any more. I'm too damn frightened. I'm not a philosopher; I don't really know whether fear is a legitimate basis for virtue. But it works for me."

"The man hasn't been born who is worth dying for. And I should know. Gerry, would you do me a favour?"

"Sure thing."

"Will you cut my hair?"

"You mean here? Now?"

"Here and now."

"No. First of all I don't have my proper tools. Second, I'd hate to do anything more than trim hair as spectacular as yours. What do you want to cut it for?"

"Several reasons. I have to find myself a job. Short hair is easier to manage. And I'm too old to wear it tumbling about my face."

Gerry put down his glass. "You're wrong on two counts. Short hair is not easy to manage. You have to keep it properly cut, and you have no options. You can't pin it up, or tie it back, or wear it in Elizabeth Barrett Browning ringlets—not that you'd want to. As for age? You're as old as whoever you're feeling. I don't know your age, Gemma girl, and I don't want to know. But you certainly aren't old enough to cut that spectacular hair."

"But, Gerry . . ."

He held up his hand. "Besides, you're tired and emotional. Read: a little bit drunk. Now is not the time to decide. Sleep on it. If tomorrow you really want to have it cut, drop by the salon anytime and I'll fit you in. Okay? Now, what are your plans?"

"In the long term: find myself a job. I'll probably go back to private cases. I don't think I'm up to ward work. But I'll have to take whatever I can get. For the short term: I have a meeting with Brian Chisholm tomorrow morning. I'm hoping to persuade him to pay Fran for her catering. I wouldn't mind if he paid me as well; I have a week's salary due. But as long as Fran gets her money I'm prepared to call it quits."

"Are you going to vamp him, as they used to say in the movies?"

I gave a rueful little laugh. "I've already tried, with zero results. He still calls me Miss Johnstone. Turns out he prefers them young. He's not quite Humbert Humbert. I don't think he's into nymphets. But he flipped over Claire."

"She's a looker, I'll have to admit. But even if I was straight I don't think she'd turn me on. Beautiful or not, she's a bit of a zombie. So's Chisholm, I'm willing to bet. I hardly said two words to him, but I could sense the disapproval. I'm one of 'those.' It's the son who has all the zip and zing. Young people today don't have all those hangups about sex we had to contend with. They believe in whatever turns you on."

Gerry put down his glass firmly and leaned forward, his eyes seeking out mine. "Gemma, my reason for coming here tonight was to make you a proposition."

"La, sir, and me an orphan."

"Not that kind of proposition, dearie, a heavy-duty one. Luc and I are thinking seriously, very seriously, of leaving Tresses and Tonsure and starting up our own salon. I know received wisdom argues against starting up a small business during a period of recession. But Luc and I aren't getting any younger; if we don't make the break now we'll run out of steam. I've always dreamed of working for myself. We both have a loyal clientele who I am sure would follow us. I know it's a gamble; we're banking on the idea that even during hard times people will pay to look their best, that they can scrape up a few bucks to stroke their vanity. It's a risk, but these days what isn't?"

"I think it sounds like a great idea. You'll never know if you don't give it a try. And I for one will remain your client."

Gerry continued. "I've been poor all my life, so the idea doesn't scare me. Luc likes to come on like a cynical bitch, but he's so middle class it hurts. He wants a condo and a microwave and a pension plan and a cottage by the lake. And he'll work hard, harder than I, to get them. But, and this is where you come in, we need a receptionist, accountant, person Friday: someone to make appointments, deal with the phone, the cash, the customers. Luc and I will have our hands full as we won't be able to afford assistants."

"Am I to assume you want me for the job?"

"Right!" Gerry clasped his hands together. "You'd be perfect. You know how to deal with people. I watched you at the party this afternoon. You were good. You're the right age; you don't look like some bimbo who was late for work because she was trapped under her boyfriend. And every morning I'd comb your hair a different way. You'd be a walking advertisement for the house." He smiled his megawatt smile. "Think of it, Gemma. Every girl dreams of working in a beauty parlour—a 'salon of beauty,' as we say in French. It's part of the collective female unconscious, like dating a movie star."

I took a reflective sip of gin. "I don't know, Gerry. As you say, it's a gamble. I love the idea, but I still have to pay the rent."

Gerry held up his hands. "All I ask is that you think it over. We're still in the planning stage. Just consider it. And please, pretty please, don't cut your hair. It's one of our major assets."

He stood. "And now I must go. Tomorrow is a long day. You know, I don't mind working long hours, but I'd far rather be working for myself."

I stood, and we moved towards the door.

"Are you upset about the old lady?" he asked.

"More than I would have thought possible. I knew her for less than a week, but I feel as though I have lost a real friend."

"Then you have. And time—days, weeks, hours—doesn't mean a thing. You can make a lasting friend in fifteen minutes if you're on the right wavelength. You know how I hate sentimentality, but at least you did get to know one another, if only briefly. That has to count for something. Not every trick develops into a big love affair, but that's no reason not to turn the trick. If you think you're better off for having known her, then it sure wasn't a wasted week."

Gerry kissed my cheek. "Now I'm off, in a cloud of dust and small stones. I'll call tomorrow."

I stood at the doorway of my apartment watching him walk briskly down the hall and into the elevator. I returned to where I had been sitting and finished my gin. To my surprise I realized I was crying. Tears, soft, saline, soothing, trickled down my cheeks. These were not the anguished, bitter tears I had wept in the taxi as I drove away from Buckingham Gardens, desperately hoping the driver was not watching me in his rear-view mirror. These tears were comfortable, cozy almost; and by the time I had wiped my eyes and blown my nose I felt washed clean. It was time to turn in. Tomorrow waited to be dealt with. I did not relish the prospect, but as I switched off the light I felt that I would be able to cope.

Thirteen

I telephoned Brian Chisholm from the hotel lobby; he stood in the opened door of his suite as I stepped off the elevator. Today I was the tailored woman; under my light overcoat I wore a black suit, charcoal pantyhose, black pumps. My hair had been pulled back and fastened at the nape. I wore no jewellery. Only a blouse of sage green silk softened the look of a middle echelon executive on the go.

Brian ushered me into the living room, furnished in the kind of calculated brocade and marble opulence designed to make the resident feel he is not merely renting a room in a hotel. He offered me a drink from the mini-bar, housed in the same elaborate armoire as the television set. I asked for a Perrier, not because I was thirsty, but to add a note of civility to an otherwise businesslike occasion.

"And now, Miss Johnstone, what can I do for you?"

As I sat, my skirt rode up over my knees. I gave it a theatrical tug, but it refused to budge. Demurely I crossed my legs at the ankles, a position which showed them off to good advantage.

"Mr. Chisholm, I spoke with Tim last night; I had hoped to attend the funeral. He told me there had been some unpleasantness."

"You might say. I had dinner with Tim last night,

possibly before your call. He told me," he paused, fighting a smile, "that there had been some unpleasantness between you and my sister."

"You might say." For a moment we both looked hard at the floor, trying not to laugh. "However, that is not why I am here. In due course I will pay my respects at the cemetery. Now, I fully realize this is not an auspicious time to discuss money, but I wanted to catch you before you left Montreal. To be brief, my friend, Fran Sullivan, has not been paid for her catering. Ordinarily I would have approached your sister, but her dislike of me is obvious. I am prepared to forego my own salary; it was only for a week after all; but I would very much like to see Mrs. Sullivan compensated for her work."

"What did she charge?"

"I don't have her receipts, but she quoted twenty dollars a head; and she prepared for thirty people. I gave her a two hundred dollar advance from money withdrawn from Mrs. Chisholm's account. Mrs. Blake has the remaining cash and my account book."

"I see." Brian spoke from his armchair, hands folded on his knee. Seen away from the context of 27 Buckingham Gardens he was much better looking than I had remembered. "That means she still has four hundred dollars coming to her. Can I give you a cheque?"

Surprised by his ready acquiescence, I could only nod. "Why, yes, that would be fine."

"Now, what about your salary? Have you been paid anything at all?"

"No, I haven't; nothing."

"What are you owed?"

I explained how Mrs. Blake had left for her cruise without settling an amount. Mrs. Chisholm had agreed to pay me nurse's scale for two regular shifts, in effect three hundred dollars a day.

"Very well. Is there anything else?"

"No, I paid for incidental expenses from Mrs. Chisholm's money. I kept track of everything spent."

Crossing to the desk, Brian clicked open his briefcase and found a chequebook. It took only seconds for him to fill out a cheque, which he handed to me. "I hope this will be satisfactory."

About to slide the pale blue rectangle into my bag, I glanced at the amount: $3000.00. "Excuse me, Mr. Chisholm, but you have overpaid me."

"Miss Johnstone, in spite of what my sister may say or think, I know how much you contributed to Mother's final days. She was an old lady; sooner or later she had to die. But she was so alive, so interested, so excited about her party. You did all you could for Mother while she was alive. Discounting my sister, the rest of us, both family and friends, are aware of how happy you made her. I shall always be grateful for what you did."

"All I did was my job. I treated her as a person, not as an invalid. Perhaps I pushed her too hard . . ."

"No, don't think that, not for a moment. She died a happy and contented woman. And for that I will always consider myself in your debt."

High praise indeed, considering the source. Could it be that away from that dreary house he too saw me in a different light? Buoyed as I was by that beautiful cheque shut safely into my handbag, I allowed myself a little rush of optimism. Could it possibly be that Brian's generosity had been motivated by his regard for me, as a woman and not just as his mother's competent companion?

Once again I flashed him my laser look, eyes wide, direct, lambent: code for "I am at your disposal."

It had not escaped my attention that after handing me the cheque, Brian remained standing. Men like Brian always stand when about to say something important. More than just thinking on their feet, they have to be on their feet in order to think. With the warm glow of anticipation I awaited his next words.

"Miss Johnstone, I have a favour to ask."

I smiled my most disingenuous smile. "Ask away."

"Do you know where I can reach Claire Laplante? She disappeared yesterday afternoon while I was at the hospital and I don't know where to find her."

How often have I read that thinking is not a precise and linear activity, but random, spontaneous, disjointed. My thoughts at that moment must have resembled ingredients in a blender spinning at full speed. In spite of the generous cheque—more of a bribe than a gratuity—Brian still thought of me as nothing more than a satisfactory employee. Furthermore, all I had to do was shake my head from side to side and my smarting vanity would be partially soothed. He would have to relinquish Claire, or hire a detective to track her down. I suspected Brian was too discreet for that kind of tactic. I had him by the short hairs.

Yet what was to be gained by withholding the truth? Claire Laplante's supposed virtue was minor compared with what a man like Brian Chisholm could do for her. We were talking about the real world. At the moment, aside from her beauty, Claire's assets were nil. Her mother was virtually unemployed. The two of them did not even have a home. Without money or backing, Claire faced a bleak future. A man like Brian could be her magic carpet into the kind of affluent, middle-class life to which we all aspire, openly or covertly. Was I, for nothing more than mere selfish bitchiness, going to deny her this opportunity? That is providing she decided to accept it.

These thoughts spun wildly through my head as Brian stood, tense, eager, waiting for my reply.

"If you know, please tell me."

His remark shattered a silence which had begun to congeal.

"She's staying with Fran Sullivan on Bedford Road. Her number is in the phone book." I did not look at him as I spoke.

"Thank you, Miss Johnstone."

"And now I must go." I reached for my coat. "I know you have a lunch engagement. Thank you, Mr. Chisholm." I offered my hand to shake, even as I averted my eyes.

"Goodbye, Miss Johnstone. I won't forget this."

I nodded and left the suite. And that was that.

As I waited for the elevator to carry me down to the lobby, I found myself wondering about my own future. For the time being I was solvent, but I could not coast indefinitely. Even if Gerry and Luc did get their act together and set up shop, there would still be delays while they found a location, negotiated a lease, redecorated, installed telephones, sent out a mailing, and much, much more. And the whole idea might turn out to be stillborn. In the meantime I had to pay my way.

The elevator door opened. Inside stood a married couple evidently in the middle of an argument. My presence shut them up, although she continued to glare at him from under pencilled brows and fibreglass hair. His normally high colour was heightened by restrained wrath. At least I had never been locked into one of those dreary, no-win relationships which people are prepared to endure because they burn up all their energy on dislike, with none left over to search for the exit.

The door opened onto the lobby; I stepped out and to one side. No sooner had they moved into the open space of the main lobby than they picked up their quarrel, probably at the precise point where they had broken off.

A figure loomed in front of me. "Gemma?"

The sheer bulk identified the figure as Tim, although the navy blue suit and striped tie made him look older.

"Hello, Tim, are you just on your way up to see your father?"

"No, I had breakfast with him. As a matter of fact, I was waiting for you. He told me you were coming to see him."

"And here I am. Are there any new developments since our conversation last night? Has your aunt changed her mind about the funeral?"

"No, unfortunately." He glanced around the populated lobby. "Could we go for a walk, somewhere we can talk privately?"

We headed for the revolving door. "Won't you be cold without an overcoat?" I asked.

"In a wool suit?" He laughed. "I'll be glad to get away from this overheated building. I'm only wearing a suit because I was having breakfast with Father and then we met with the family lawyer."

We began to stroll along Sherbrooke Street. "You have something you wanted to discuss?" I asked.

"Yes. I'm looking for a place to live. I have a roommate, sort of a nerd, but he's all right, I guess. He has this girlfriend who wants to move to Montreal so they can live together. The apartment isn't big enough for two, let alone three, and I'd like to move anyway. I was wondering if I could move into your second bedroom, and we could split the rent."

For a moment I was sorely tempted by the idea of sharing

costs. That way I could probably manage to keep on the apartment. But the idea of Tim underfoot was daunting.

"I don't know, Tim. I'm awfully used to being on my own. What happens if I meet a man I like? You would have the same problem all over again."

He grinned at me. "Not if I'm that man."

A number of body blows had temporarily dulled my reflexes. "I beg your pardon?"

"I said—not if I'm that man. You have a king size bed. That's good because I take up a lot of room. And those nights you want to sleep alone I can use the other bedroom."

The coin dropped. "Just a minute, Tim. Are you suggesting what I think you are suggesting?"

"Yes," he replied without commentary.

"Tim, I'm old enough to be your mother."

"But you're not my mother."

Unable to refute his logic, I fell silent from sheer astonishment. Seizing the advantage, Tim stopped walking, obliging me to stop as well.

"I thought you were incredibly hot when I saw you in that gold dress. Then, as I got to know you better, I realized how much I really liked you. We actually talked to one another." He burst out laughing. "And then, yesterday afternoon, when you tripped Aunt Christine. . . Wow! All my life I've wanted to do something rude to Aunt Christine, like making her an apple pie filled with kitty litter, or putting Saran Wrap over her toilet bowl. But I'm supposed to be a gentleman and she is my aunt. So when I watched you let her have it—it was as if you were playing out my fantasy for me."

I smiled. "You know, Tim, your aunt may not be my favourite

person, but losing your mother and having your marriage break up—and all in one weekend—is enough to sour anyone's disposition." I looked directly at him. "But this is the first time you have mentioned that, that I was anything other than a friend."

"True enough. I wanted to wait until you realized Dad was out of bounds. I could see you had your eye on him, and I can't blame you. He's got a lot going for him. But Dad likes chicks. That's why Mother left him. I guess he and I are two sides of the coin, because I happen to like older women. They know what you are doing without having to be told. By now you must have realized Dad has a thing for Claire. He tried to find out from me, indirectly of course, where she was. I don't know, but I suspect he got the information from you. If not, he'll still find her. He is incredibly single-minded. So there you are, Gemma; you may be too old for Father, but you're the right age for me."

I didn't know whether to be angry or amused. Anger takes more energy than laughter, and I was a little bit punchy. I started to giggle.

"Aside from the fact that I'm still old enough to be your mother, what will your father say about your bunking in with me?"

"He won't care. With Claire on his mind he won't have time. And I just earned myself a lot of brownie points. We cut a deal over breakfast. I agreed to go to law school for one year. If I really dislike it, then I will be free to study whatever I like."

"You appear to have everything neatly worked out."

"Naturally. When making a major change, the less you leave to chance the more likely you are to succeed."

In spite of my better judgement I couldn't help wondering what it would be like to make love to all that youth and bulk and energy. Common sense told me to retreat, but common sense is not nearly so plausible as commonly supposed. Uncertain of what to say, I started to walk. Tim fell into step beside me. Someone had obviously told him a gentleman walks on the side nearest the road, and I confess a weakness for good manners.

"Look," he said, "let's have lunch and talk it over. You have to eat and we passed the Ritz only a minute ago. How about it?"

"The Ritz is expensive, Tim. The last time I ate there was with your grandmother."

He reached for my arm. "All the more reason to return. We'll order wine and drink a toast to Gran. I know she would have approved. As for money?" He reached into his trouser pocket and produced a wad of bills that would have choked a boa constrictor. "I managed to get an advance on my inheritance, part of the deal I made with Dad. And there's plenty more where that came from."

As I looked at the money, taupe, pink, olive, resting in his enormous hand, I felt the old sensation the sight of money invariably brings on, a kind of pleasant tingle in what my mother would have called "the naughty bits." On top of which I had not enjoyed male company since Walter died. I had not eaten any breakfast, and the idea of food was very appealing.

"All right, Tim, we'll have lunch, and a bottle of wine, and toast your grandmother. Then? We'll see."

"Fair enough. But before we go into the dining room, would you mind unfastening your hair so it falls onto your shoulders? I like it best that way."

His smile warmed me right down to my ankles. I took his arm and we retraced our steps to the canopy. It really would be a good idea for me to eat something. And I certainly had no urgent plans for the rest of the afternoon.